CALL OF DREAM

The Swords and Beasts of Gardoon

SCORPION KING TALE

INDIA · SINGAPORE · MALAYSIA

ISBN 979-8-89363-285-9

Disclaimer

This book is a work of fiction. All characters, events, and incidents portrayed in this novel are products of the author's imagination. Any resemblance to actual persons, living or dead, or real events is purely coincidental.

The author acknowledges that certain themes, emotions, and experiences depicted in the story may resonate with readers on a personal level. However, it is important to emphasize that this work is a creative endeavor and should not be interpreted as reflecting any real-life individuals or occurrences.

Readers are encouraged to enjoy the story for its entertainment value and the imaginative world it presents.

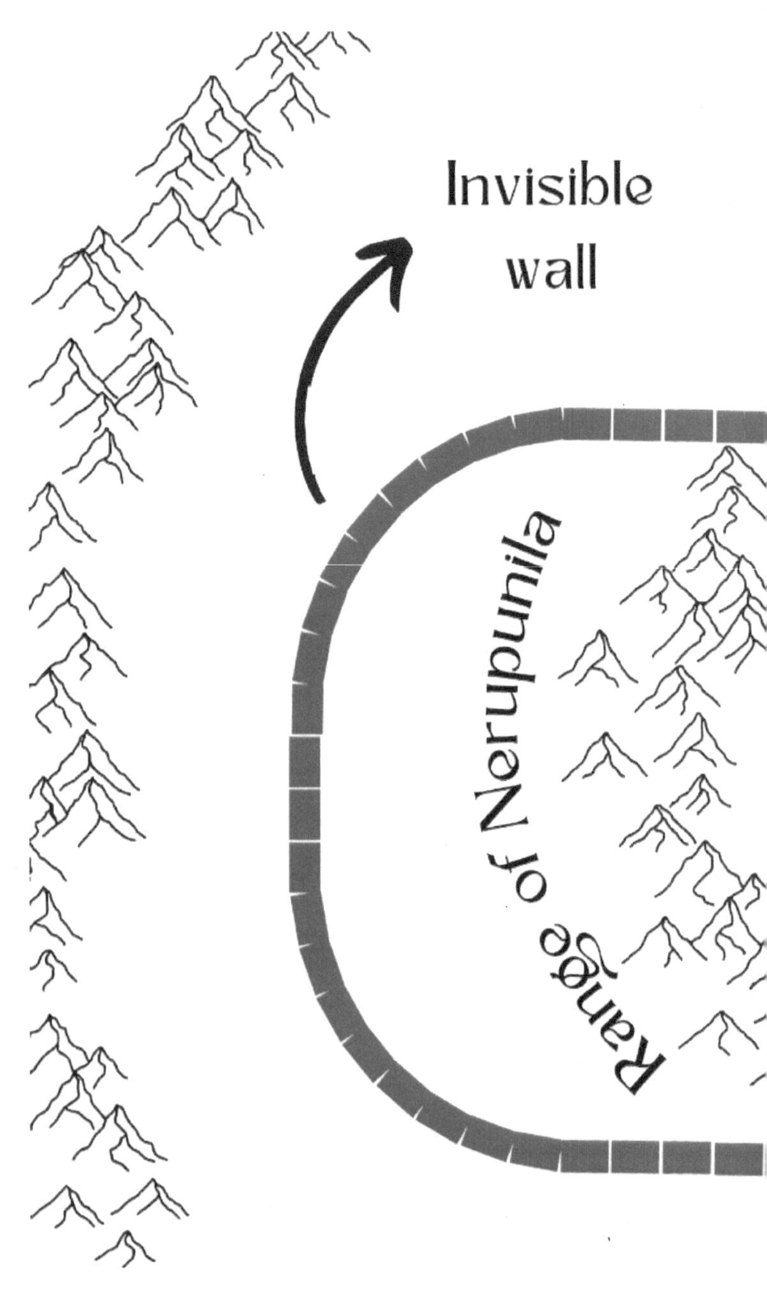
Invisible
wall
Range of Nerupunila

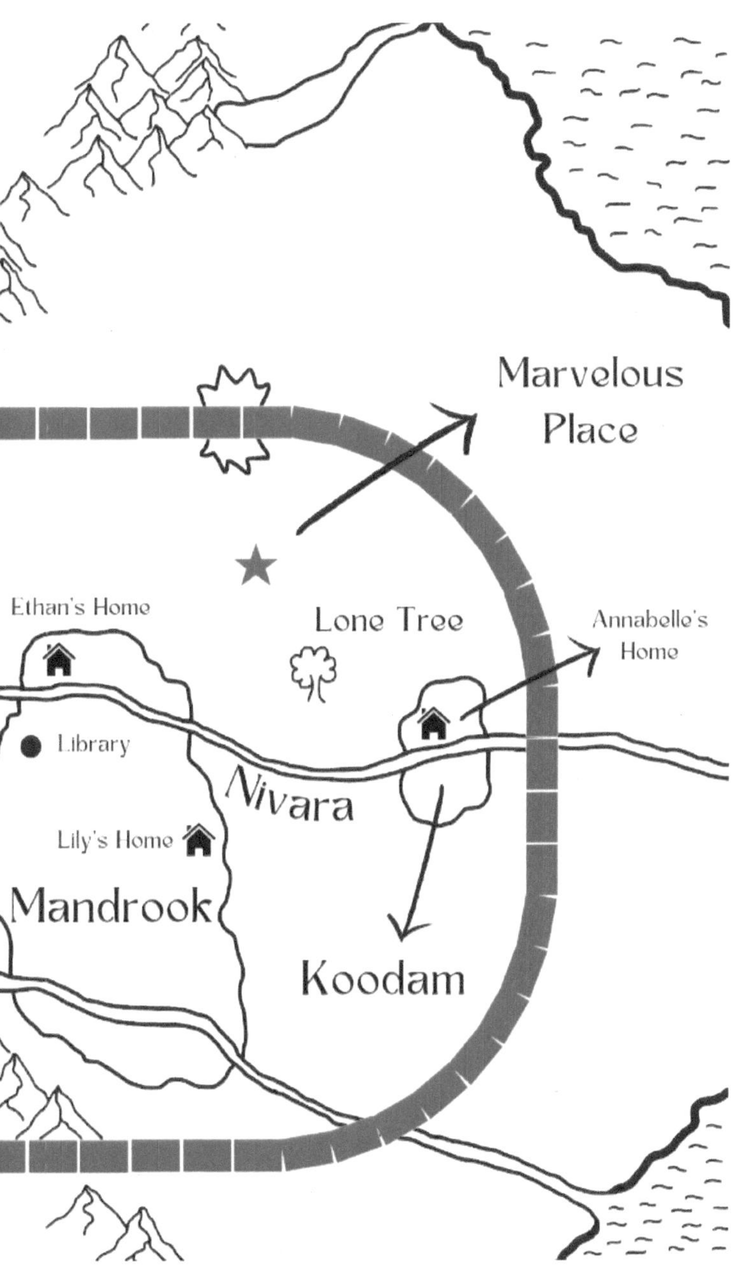
Marvelous
Place
Ethan's Home
Lone Tree
Annabelle's
Home
Library
Nivara
Lily's Home
Mandrook
Koodam

Contents

Acknowledgments

I would also like to acknowledge the countless authors, researchers, and thinkers whose works have paved the way for my own. Your contributions to the field have been a constant source of inspiration and knowledge.

I extend my gratitude to my readers. Your interest in my work fuels my passion to continue writing and exploring new ideas.

This book would not have been possible without the support and encouragement of all these wonderful individuals. Thank you for being a part of this journey.

With heartfelt appreciation,

Scorpion King Tale.

Inference

Humans are not to be taken for granted; our brains have immense capabilities and mysteries that are hard to figure out. Look at the things around you. Most of them were made by the human mind, using our precious gifts – Thoughts, Imagination, and Subconscious. If the human mind itself is not to be taken for granted, then think of the power that created the human mind, the power that made the existence of life possible, the power from which the stars came, the power of nature. It goes beyond our imagination and understanding to realize the true reason for our existence.

The elements of nature are so powerful that they make life possible on a planet. The one who possesses the power to control the elements of nature can bring chaos under control but at the same time can unleash destruction on a huge scale. How would the world be if it had people who could control the elements?

Legends say that everything that happens around us has a reason. The reason, though, is hard to figure out. The one who awakens their best self is the one whom the world would love and fear.

Prologue

In a distant universe called Kan, a few trillion light years away from the Milky Way Galaxy, lies a planet named Gardoon. Kan is much older than our own universe. Gardoon boasts of a climate similar to that of the Earth, making it conducive to life.

Over time, the evolution of Gardoon gave rise to humans, the planet's most intelligent inhabitants. However, Gardoon is also home to colossal creatures, some of which possess magical abilities. They can control the elements of nature, other animals, even good and bad energies, and much more. These creatures once ruled Gardoon until humans emerged. With their sixth sense, humans gained control of Gardoon, surpassing the magical creatures in intellect.

Though humans eventually learned to coexist with the colossal beings, darkness began to corrupt some individuals, leading them to seek out cruel practices to extract the creatures' magic, in turn killing them.

As darkness threatened to consume Gardoon, God-like beings known as Devarnams, who oversee the planet's well-being, sought aid from similar beings from other worlds in Kan. Together, they fought the darkness in the War of Nalvil, containing but not defeating it entirely.

The Devarnams must ready Gardoon for the darkness's inevitable return. They work to ensure the planet can withstand this powerful threat.

After the war, Thiarral, the head of Devarnams of Gardoon, investigated the cause of the darkness's release in the first place. Shockingly, he discovered his beloved son, Garvil, was involved, along with Thiarral's wife, Kaiya, and Garvil's love, Vaulmour. Out of all his sons and daughters, he liked and valued Garvil the most. He was heartbroken by the recent discovery of betrayal.

Every Devarnams thought that Thiarral would go easy on his wife and his favorite son. But despite his affection, he did not show mercy. He was furious at their betrayal and misuse of their powers and responsibilities. Thiarral punished them by reducing them to a lesser life form, making them three-dimensional beings in Gardoon. This was their chance to learn the importance of their responsibilities.

Kaiya, the creator of life in Gardoon, shaped the world's nature with her elegance. When she was sent to live on Gardoon, her daughter Ira stepped into her role. Meanwhile, Garvil, tasked with purifying souls, found his position filled by his brother, Zendayan, though nobody could replace him perfectly.

Thiarral, aided by Devarnams from other worlds, erected an invisible wall around two towns, Mandrook and Koodam, to protect a powerful artifact from the darkness. If the darkness obtained this artifact, it would spell disaster for Gardoon.

The people of Mandrook and Koodam were under a magic spell, unaware of the wall's existence, ensuring the artifact's protection remained a secret.

Chapter 1

Smile, Nature, Not Normal

About 1200 years had passed since the end of the War of Nalvil.

In the magical world of Gardoon existed the bustling town of Mandrook, where smog choked the skyline, and trash littered the streets and water bodies. Mandrook and its neighboring town, Koodam had an invisible wall around them that protected the towns and made them invisible to the rest of Gardoon. Unaware of the impending dangerous events for his town, Ethan was sleeping on his bed.

Ethan was an ordinary college student living a normal life in Mandrook, but there was one extraordinary thing about his life that consumed his thoughts day and night. Her name was Lily, a girl in his class, whose every glance, and every word were etched in his heart like a secret he could not wait to share.

For months, Ethan had admired Lily from afar, enchanted by her radiant smile, her graceful stride, and the way her laughter seemed to brighten even the gloomiest of days. But Ethan was a shy and introverted young man, and the mere thought of speaking to her sent waves of nervousness through his veins.

Every morning, as he walked to his college, his heart raced with anticipation. He tried to devise the perfect plan to approach Lily, to say something clever, or funny that would make her notice him. He stayed up late at night, brainstorming ideas, crafting witty remarks, and even rehearsing his lines in front of the mirror. Yet, when he saw her in the hallways or during class, his voice would falter, and his courage would wane.

As he continued this internal struggle, something else began to occupy his thoughts. On his daily walk to college, he could not help but notice the extent of environmental degradation that had engulfed the city. Plastic bags danced like spectral apparitions in the wind, smog hung in the air like a veil of despair, and the once-pristine river, Nivara, that flowed through the city had transformed into a sludge-filled wasteland. It was as if nature itself was mourning the town's demise.

One fateful day in his classroom, Lily's words struck him like a bolt of lightning. She said that she was organizing community clean-up events, starting recycling initiatives, and planting trees to replace the gloomy, concrete jungle with pockets of greenery. Ethan knew it was his ticket for both his wishes to come true.

With the courage that he was unaware of, he stood up and volunteered to help Lily.

His heart melted and his mind jumped as he saw Lily look at him and smile. The cuteness in the curves made by her lips and cheeks; the one thing he had been yearning for the most, the opportunity to see her smile up close, had at last become a reality!

Not only did his bravery bring a smile to Lily's face, but it also drew the attention of some of his classmates. Unconcerned about the stares, he maintained his focus on what truly mattered to him.

That evening when he was walking back home, he heard some voice calling his name from behind him. He saw some of his classmates had followed him. He was not surprised to see the same stares that he saw that morning. He could not help but notice that he was perfectly in a place where his cry for help would not be noticed.

He knew the boys were there to warn him about getting close to Lily. Ethan stood without a word. He had observed Lily closely enough to know that her heart remained unclaimed by anyone. While he held confidence in his capability to outrun the boys, if need be, a seed of doubt lingered in the back of his mind. He spoke to himself, advising him not to do anything stupid. He did the math in his mind and did not see a winning chance in a fight. As he was devising a perfect response, he heard a honk.

The windows rolled down from a black sedan and a woman spoke, "Do any of you boys know the way to Mr. Soleman's house?"

Ethan looked at the woman and said, "I know and I can help you reach faster if you can give me a ride."

The woman said, "Sure, young man. Hop in!"

Ethan walked past the boys staring at him to get inside the car. The woman realized that there had been an argument among the boys and Ethan had used the opportunity to escape from the situation by getting in her car. She stepped on the accelerator and followed the directions communicated by Ethan.

The woman asked, "May I know your name, young man?"

Ethan introduced himself and said that Mr. Soleman's house was just on the corner of the street on which they were driving.

Thanking him for guiding her, the woman then asked about the location of his house, intending to drop him off. Ethan said, "Earlier while introducing myself, I might have missed mentioning my last name. My full name is Ethan Soleman."

The woman looked at Ethan in surprise and asked, "Are you Thomas Soleman and Emma Soleman's son?"

Ethan nodded his head. The woman introduced herself as Ella Watson. She was enthusiastic to uncover that piece of information about Ethan. She said that she was a very good friend of his parents and that she had last seen him when he was very young. She said that she had a misunderstanding related to work with his parents and thus, they hadn't met for several years.

Everything that Ella said after introducing herself faded away as Ethan was fixated on Ella's second name. Ethan interrupted Ella's conversation as Ella stopped in front of his house. Ethan asked, "Are you by any chance related to Lily Watson?"

Ella said, "Yeah, Lily is my daughter. How do you know Lily?"

Ethan said, "Lily and I go to the same college, we're classmates." With an appreciative smile directed at Ella, he thanked her as she and Lily both graciously shared the same smile and eyes.

Ella felt a tinge of warmth in her heart on hearing Ethan's words. She said, "I hope your parents welcome me with the same warmth."

She turned towards his house and tears dropped from one of her eyes as she remembered the things from the past. She quickly wiped her tears as she did not want Ethan to see her crying.

Ethan ran to the door and pressed the doorbell. He turned back to see Ella hesitant to walk towards the door. The door opened and Emma saw Ella. Ethan, without noticing the door being open, called out for Ella, welcoming her into his house. He turned to his mother, said that they had a guest, and ran upstairs to his room.

Ella walked towards the door and saw Emma staring at her and asked, "Hi Emma, how are you?"

Emma said, "For the allegations you made against us and the words that you spoke to us in the past, I would not have let you inside my house. But somehow you were accompanied by my son and he invited you in. So, you are welcome this time. But if you are here to hurt us more, then please return. We cannot bear any more false claims."

Ella looked into Emma's eyes and said, "Believe me. I am not here to hurt anyone."

Ethan ran to his room, changed his clothes, and came down to the kitchen as he wanted something to eat. He saw his mother hugging Ella. He felt happy as they got along because the issue between his parents and Lily's parents would have been a show-stopper for his dream to win Lily's heart. He did not want to disturb their talk as it seemed like it was important. So, he proceeded to the kitchen and got some bread and peanut butter.

Having finished his snack, he was on his way back to his room, when he saw Ella's smile as she was leaving their house. The glimpse of her smile served as a catalyst, reigniting the memory of Lily's enchanting smile from that morning, now etched deeply in his mind. Strangely, as he mentally replayed the morning incident, the happiness he felt seemed to intensify, surpassing even the joy of the actual moment.

He went to his room and began thinking about the things he could do to get Lily's attention. He spent the evening completely dedicated to achieving his goal in life. He got many ideas as he put his mind to them. The small distractions around were nothing compared to his aim, so they became weak and vanished.

He wrote down the initial draft of a perfect plan to save the environment and spend more time with Lily. He felt proud of himself. He congratulated himself for coming up with such an idea.

Full of happiness, he went down for his dinner. He found his parents were not as happy as they used to be. He asked them if everything was alright. His mother said that there was nothing to worry about and that their problem need not affect him.

Thomas asked Ethan about his day and how he met Ella.

Ethan began saying that he had one of the best days of his life. He shared that his bicycle's chain had unexpectedly broken, compelling him to leave it for repairs at a service center conveniently positioned on his way to college. In the evening, he went back to the service center but they said that the owner of the place had left the town due to a personal emergency, so he could not get his bicycle back. He mentioned that as he was heading home, he encountered Ella seeking assistance along the way to his house.

Thomas asked, "I thought you said you had the best day of your life."

Ethan explained, "Even though I faced some challenges, making someone smile in college made it the best day for me. That single smile made me forget all the troubles I had."

Emma looked at Thomas and asked, "Ella had been a frequent visitor to our house before our argument in the past. She must be aware of the location of our house, so why did she ask for Ethan's help?"

Thomas said, "Hmm… Yeah. It did not cross my mind. But maybe it is because of the way this part of the town has changed. I noted that she mentioned that she had not been to this part of the town lately. That could be the reason. Moreover, almost all the houses in our street are of the same design. In the first few weeks, when we moved to this house, even I found it difficult to differentiate our house."

Emma nodded her head agreeing with Thomas. She looked at Thomas and said, "I am worried."

Ethan wanted to know if his mother was fine with Ella's sudden appearance in their lives. He did not want anything to go wrong between his parents and Lily's parents.

He asked, "Anything that I need to be worried about?"

Emma said, "Not now. Everything will pass. I hope the worry in my mind also passes."

After dinner, Ethan went up to his room and saw his plan written in his notebook. But it did not excite him as it did earlier. He closed the notebook and sat down to think. He wondered why his emotions were different now. He thought about how he was feeling before going to dinner and after he came back. He figured the sadness he saw in his parents could be the reason for his emotional shift. Then he focused his thoughts on the time when he came up with that plan. He felt like he was not himself at the time of forming the plan. He felt like he was thinking and acting like someone superior. Someone with a cause and dedication towards an aim.

He thought about what he wanted to achieve and read the plan in his notebook. Now he felt happy. He felt the pride that he felt before dinner. Sitting in his room, he realized the power of the human mind and how it is affected by emotions. Yet, a strong doubt lingered in the back of his mind. He doubted his ability to accomplish the things he planned to do.

When it was time for bed, he turned off the lights and lay down on his bed. His body was not too tired as he had not been doing much physical activity and had not been doing his workouts for a couple of weeks. So, he did not immediately go to sleep as soon as he closed his eyes.

He began thinking about the events that took place that day. About the incidents being perfectly executed. He thought about the time and place where his cycle's chain broke.

It happened right in the middle of the bridge that connected the other side of the town over the plastic-filled filth river. That was the place where he felt bad about the environment as he had seen a fish that was caught in a plastic bag and was struggling to breathe.

The fish reminded him about his sister who had drowned in that river when she was young. He could not do anything to help the fish except watch it suffocate and die. But instead of feeling bad for that fish, he wanted to think of a way to prevent other fish from dying that way.

On his walk to his college, he was constantly thinking about the river. He wanted to do something to make it better. Due to this thought in his mind, he immediately showed his support for Lily's initiative and got a beautiful gift from nature in the form of her smile.

Lily's smile was the most beautiful expression he had seen on Lily's face. He fell asleep in happiness and had a dream about Lily.

In his dream, he was standing in the middle of a garden filled with flower blossoms. He felt like he could hear someone cry. He turned around but could see no one. He was alone in the garden. He could not find anyone. He began walking around and saw a woman sitting on the ground, weeping. He walked towards her and began to speak.

Suddenly he was stunned to feel someone touching his shoulders from behind him. He turned around quickly and saw Lily. She was wearing a red dress, looking at him, and smiling. He could see love in her eyes. They both locked their eyes and Lily moved toward him to kiss him.

Ethan, who had not kissed a girl before in his life, was unsure about how to proceed at that moment. He saw Lily leaning towards him with her eyes closed. He saw her lips and forgot about his fear and the weeping girl. He closed his eyes to completely enjoy his kiss. Before closing his eyes, he placed his hands softly on the sides of her face to approximately know the position of her lips.

He waited for her soft lips to touch his lips, but he was shocked as the kiss landed on his forehead. He opened his eyes to see Lily kiss his forehead. He was in a different garden now. He was sitting on the ground and Lily was sitting beside him. Her smile was unbeatable. The breeze and the Sun made it better. He was overwhelmed with love and hugged her, resting his face on her shoulder. He could feel the warmth.

He was happy until he felt something weird. He felt the presence of something bright. He lifted his head from Lily's shoulder and found himself in a different garden. The Sun had almost set and the night had started spreading its wings. He was not sitting on the ground but standing and Lily was standing beside him to his left, holding his hands tight, looking at something curious. The brightness of the thing that she was looking at was shining in her eyes. Lily looked at him and then back at the bright light.

Ethan turned to look at the light, but he could not see anything as the light was too bright for human eyes. He could not comprehend the thing that he was looking at. He had never seen something like that. The light's intensity and brightness increased with every second. At some point, the light's intensity was so high that it made both of them close their eyes.

He maintained a firm grip on Lily's hand, refusing to let go, and she reciprocated with an equally strong grasp. The light was so bright that he had to use his other hand to cover his eyes. He tried looking at the light, hoping to figure out what was causing it. He felt some movement. It felt like the source of the light was dancing.

He felt sorrow and anger at the same time in the movement of the light. Somehow he knew that the slow movement of the light represented sorrow and the intensity of the light represented rage. He felt that someone or something that was producing the light was not happy about something.

Suddenly he felt someone touching his right hand, just above his elbow. He turned to his right and saw a girl. She was struggling to look at the light and was closing her eyes with her hands. As her hands were not efficient enough to block the light, she buried her face into Ethan's arm to protect her eyes from the light. Ethan could not figure out who the girl was as he could not see her face properly. But he did not want to disturb her by attempting to look at her face.

The light's brightness kept increasing. Ethan could feel the heat increasing. It reached a point where he could not bear the heat. He was struggling a lot and then suddenly the light got dimmer. He tried looking at the light to figure out the source. The light began to take form. He felt a sense of relaxation. He felt like the source of the light had figured out a solution for its sorrow. As an effect, its movement became faster and its anger reduced, in turn reducing its light's intensity. He was fixated on the light but could not figure out what it was. He saw a beam of orangish yellow light shoot into the sky.

He was disturbed as he felt like he heard someone laughing from behind him. It was a woman's voice. He immediately turned around and as he did, he woke up from his dream the next morning. Relief washed over him as he realized it was just a dream, freeing him from the need to figure out the mystery of the light. It was all in his imagination. He felt a bit disappointed because he had hoped that the parts about Lily were real.

He sat on his bed and looked at his alarm clock. The clock hands were just about to hit six. He waited a couple of minutes for the alarm to go off before getting up from his bed. He turned the alarm off as soon as it began ringing, and with a smile on his face, he went to brush his teeth. While bathing, he felt an unusual silence. He could not hear anything except the sound of the water falling on the floor. It caught his attention, especially because he could not hear any birds chipping.

He walked to the living hall downstairs and saw his father sitting on the couch with his hands raised. Initially, he thought that his father was stretching a bit. But even after a while, he did not drop his hands below. It started to get weirder, so he asked his father about his hands being raised. But his father did not respond to him, he seemed too fixated on his breathing. So, he did not ask him many questions and thought it was a prank.

He headed to the kitchen to see what his mother was preparing for breakfast. He saw his mother preparing breakfast with her left hand holding the vessel's handle and the right hand holding onto a spoon to stir and cook the vegetables in the vessel. He began talking to his mother to know if she was feeling alright as he remembered his mother being sad the previous night. His mother did not respond but instead turned her gaze toward him and smiled.

Ethan's thoughts were conquered by hunger as his stomach started growling. He asked her how long would it take for the breakfast to be ready. On hearing that, his mother picked up a fruit, washed it, and handed it to him. He took the fruit from his mother's right hand.

He noticed that her left hand was raised in the air. As soon as he got the fruit from his mother's right hand, she raised her right hand as well.

Ethan laughed and asked, "What kind of a prank is this?"

His mother did not talk. She continued to cook. Ethan laughed and asked, "What is the purpose of this prank?"

His mother still did not talk back. So, he left saying, "Let's see for how long you both can manage to keep your hands up and not talk."

On his way to the dining table, he saw his father with his hands raised and threw the fruit towards him asking him to catch it. Surprisingly, his father caught the fruit with his right hand and handed it back to Ethan. His left hand was raised the whole time.

Ethan laughed and said, "This year's award for the best prankster parents goes to, Mr. and Mrs. Soleman!" Ethan clapped his hands and cheered.

Surprisingly, his parents did not break from their act. He became curious about their actions. For a moment he wondered if it indeed was a prank.

Ethan was amazed at his father's reflexes as he sat at the dining table to eat the fruit. After eating, he went to the living room and watched his father's dedication towards a prank. He maintained silence and was waiting for his father to break his act. Deciding to test his father's dedication, he thought if he left the house and entered quietly without making any noise, he could fool his father and catch him red-handed.

So, he informed his parents that he was leaving the house to get some fresh air and stepped out. He left the door slightly open for him to sneak inside as the main door of his house would make a noise that could collapse his plan.

He thought of waiting only for five seconds before entering inside. The five seconds were enough for him to be terrified.

The five seconds made him realize that his parents were not involved in a prank.

The five seconds caused a lot of confusion in his mind.

The five seconds made his heart pump faster in fear.

He did not understand what was happening to his parents as he saw people walking on the street, carrying on with their normal activities with their hands raised.

He stepped inside the house to the living room. His mother came out of the kitchen and straight to the dining table and began arranging their breakfast. Ethan noticed that when his mother had something in her hand, she was walking normally, but while walking back empty-handed she walked with her hands raised.

He could not possibly understand why his parents and his neighbors were raising their hands when they did not use their hands for any purpose.

As soon as his mother arranged the breakfast on the dining table, his father walked towards Ethan with his hands raised. He used his right hand to tap on Ethan's shoulder and asked him to join him for breakfast.

Chapter 2

A Series of Puzzling Events

Ethan was surprised by his father's unusual behavior, accurately predicting when his mother finished setting up breakfast without her calling him. This was a significant change from his father's habits and it added to the peculiar happenings of the day.

At the dining table, Ethan found his parents already seated with their hands raised, waiting for him to join them for breakfast. They remained silent, observing him. Ethan wondered why they were staring at him without eating.

Both his mother and father gestured for him to start eating, still with their hands raised. Ethan looked at his well-balanced meal, containing the right proportions of carbohydrates, protein, fiber, fat, vitamins, and minerals. Millions of questions raced through his mind, but the signals from his stomach to his brain, notifying him of hunger, overtook all other thoughts. Once he took a bite, his parents lowered their hands and began eating.

During breakfast, his mother suddenly stood up, took Ethan's empty glass, and went to the kitchen. Ethan, nearly finished with his meal, wondered why she took his glass as his mother returned with the glass filled with water. He was just two minutes away from completing his breakfast and did not feel thirsty. She placed it in front of him, exactly where she had taken it from, and smiled. Then, she resumed eating. Shortly after, Ethan experienced a hiccup. To his surprise, he drank the water his mother had just refilled, leaving him puzzled about how she knew about his hiccup in advance.

After breakfast, Ethan's parents sat on the couch with their hands raised. Confused, Ethan asked, "Can't you both talk?"

His parents shook their heads horizontally. He continued, "Do you know what's happening to you?" Again, they shook their heads. "Do you know why your hands are raised?"

Once more, they shook their heads. Perplexed, Ethan said, "I don't understand anything. What should I do now?"

His parents smiled and his father handed him a note. It read, "Be patient. Everything is happening for a greater good reason. Be calm and trust the process. You will get what you want."

Feeling uncertain, Ethan looked at his parents and inquired, "What do I want?"

His parents smiled, stood up, patted his shoulder and back, and then went about their tasks. His mother headed to the kitchen, and his father left the house.

Ethan followed his father outside and noticed an unusual calmness in his usually bustling street. It was very quiet, with only the sounds of wind and footsteps. Surprisingly, there were no cars around, and people were walking, or using bicycles instead.

He tried talking to people, but they seemed unresponsive. Accidentally slipping, he was caught by a stranger who helped him stand, smiled, and continued with their work. It felt like they knew he was there and understood what was going to happen to him.

Everyone was busy, and his father joined a group cleaning the streets in an organized manner, separating biodegradable, and non-biodegradable waste. People on bicycles carried the collected waste away.

Thinking of his bicycle, Ethan wanted to retrieve it for faster travel. Feeling lost, he noticed everyone around him engaged in similar activities. Wanting to find someone like him, he ran to the service center where he had left his bicycle the day before. On the way, he observed everyone contributing to the community work.

He wondered if he was dreaming and his brain was being overly creative. However, he realized it could not be a regular dream because everything felt real, and there was a logical order to the events. He knew he was not dreaming.

Ethan quickly ran to find his bicycle, ready for him to ride. He decided to go to his college, hoping to find someone who seemed normal. Upon reaching the college, he shouted to get a response but was met with silence. Just as he was about to give up, he spotted his psychology professor moving around in a wheelchair, not holding his hands up like others.

Ethan ran towards his professor and was out of breath by the time he reached him. The professor's legs were paralyzed due to a childhood accident. He remained still in his wheelchair. Ethan tried talking to him, asking questions about the strange occurrences around him.

His professor remained silent and still. Ethan thought that maybe his professor was also under control. Confirming his suspicion, the professor smiled, offering Ethan a bar of dark chocolate in a red wrapper and a white rose from his lap, which he had covered using his hands. It was a daily routine for the professor to write a word on a piece of paper and give a chocolate bar to the first person who said that specific word.

Ethan received the chocolate and rose, thinking about his long-standing desire to participate in the professor's daily ritual. Doubtful, he asked if he had spoken the word the professor had decided that morning. The professor nodded, reaching into his front shirt pocket to hand Ethan a folded piece of paper. Unfolding it, Ethan read the word 'happening' on the outside and found a positive message inside: "Everything that had happened, happened for good. What is happening now, is happening for good. All that is yet to happen, will happen for good."

After reading the message, Ethan felt confused. Something seemed off. First, his professor usually gave chocolate wrapped in white, but that day it was red. Additionally, his professor, who claimed not to like roses, gave him a white one. Ethan pondered this as he gently placed the rose in his shirt pocket and tucked the piece of paper and chocolate into his pants pocket.

He waited for a while in his college, hoping someone would come in search of those who are normal like him without their hands being raised. But no one did. Realizing there was no point in staying, he decided to leave.

On his way back home, Ethan reflected on the strange occurrences. As he passed houses, he observed women cleaning their homes and gardens. A boy from his class approached him with his hands down, but his excitement waned when he saw the boy carrying water bottles. The boy was among those who could have roughed him up the day before, had it not been for Lily's mother asking for directions to his house. The classmate handed him two small water bottles and returned home with his hands raised.

Curious about the water bottles, Ethan continued towards his house. On his way, he saw a beautiful male peacock dead in the middle of the road. He wondered what could have killed it. Looking around, no one seemed to have noticed the dead peacock, as no one bothered to give it a proper burial. Ethan thought to himself that there might be a reason the peacock was dead, and it was his responsibility to bury it.

There was something unusual about the peacock. Unlike the usual vibrant ones, it was dull-colored, with a hint of gold mixed into its plumage.

He searched for a proper place to bury the peacock. As he looked around, he found a woman walking towards him with a shovel. She approached him, both hands holding the shovel, and with her head, and neck movement, she signaled for him to follow her. She marked a rectangular area near a tree with the shovel, pushed the shovel into the sandy ground, and then left the place with her hands raised.

The doubt about him needing to bury the peacock was clarified by her actions. Ethan started digging the hole, which took him about thirty minutes. When the hole was around three feet deep, he carried the peacock to its grave and gently placed it inside the hole. He prayed for the peacock to have a better life in its next life or the afterlife and began covering the grave with mud. Just before he finished closing the grave, a woman came to him with a red rose plant. He understood what needed to be done. He planted the rose and got up with a satisfying sense in his heart.

Feeling low on energy, he decided to take a break. He sat on the pavement and realized that the tree beside which he had buried the peacock was the same one with the crow's nest on it. Watching the crows build their nest on his way to college was a routine he had developed since a crow droppings incident on his head a week ago. Thoughts about how crows build nests and share food crossed his mind, unintentionally leading him to compare them to the cooperative behavior of the people working together in the neighborhood.

Feeling thirsty, he took a sip from the water bottle in his hand. The Sun was at its peak, right on top of his head. He observed an old man walking normally with a stick in one hand and the other hand not raised. He almost did not notice the old man's hand not being raised and when he did, he was excited. He left his bicycle and ran towards the old man, eager to start a conversation. Before Ethan could speak, the old man noticed him and chuckled.

The old man asked, "Ah, boy… You have come. Did you bring it?"

Ethan found it peculiar that the old man, in his eighties, and a stranger to him, spoke as if he expected Ethan's visit. Given the recent unusual events, Ethan was less surprised, though he remained unaware of what the old man was referring to.

Politely, Ethan said, "Sorry, sir, but I'm not sure what you're asking for."

Suddenly, the old man coughed, losing balance. Ethan quickly caught him, preventing a fall. Grateful, the old man thanked him and explained, "I was asking for the chocolate and the white rose."

With a hint of doubt, Ethan retrieved the chocolate from his pocket. The old man's face lit up at the sight of the chocolate with the red wrapper. Expressing his gratitude, the old man accepted the chocolate and rose, thanked Ethan, and continued walking.

After a few steps, the old man coughed again. Concerned, Ethan offered to accompany him and offered a water bottle. The old man, in a rush, initially refused, but Ethan insisted. Getting the chocolate and rose from the old man, Ethan handed the water bottle, ensuring the old man drank it without any mishaps.

Curious, Ethan asked, "May I know your name, sir?"

The old man shared that his name was Sebastian and that he was heading to meet his wife. Ethan took back the water bottle and accompanied Sebastian. They reached a park where Sebastian sat on a bench. Ethan joined him and asked if he wanted to rest before meeting his wife.

Sebastian explained, "My dear wife passed away thirty-four days ago. Since then, life has become unbearable. With no children and no one to care for, each day is a struggle without her. I miss her smile terribly. I've prayed for God to take me to her, but he hasn't accepted me yet."

He looked at the confusion in Ethan's eyes and said, "You might be wondering why I'm sitting in a park instead of visiting her grave. Although her body is buried elsewhere, this park is where we shared many moments. I feel her presence here."

Ethan was absorbing the fact that Sebastian's wife was dead and pondered upon the reason why he said he was waiting there to see his deceased wife.

Sebastian believed he saw his wife and addressed her, saying, "Oh! There she is. She has arrived." Ethan did not see anyone around. Sebastian used his support stick to stand and interact with someone only he could see. Ethan realized Sebastian was imagining his wife's presence. Sebastian introduced Ethan as the boy who helped him, and Ethan's attempts to convince him otherwise were unsuccessful.

Sebastian affectionately said, "My Rose, you look forty years younger than me. I've brought you your favorites."

On saying that, Sebastian handed the chocolate and the white flower to his wife, and Ethan, unsure of what to do, watched. To his amazement, the white rose, and chocolate seemed to hover briefly in the air before falling to the ground. Though stunned, Ethan quickly dismissed it, thinking it might be his imagination.

Sebastian expressed, "I have been waiting for this day," dropping his support stick and extending his hands as if someone were holding them. As he took a step forward, he began to fall. Ethan rushed to catch him, explaining that there was no one in front of him, but Sebastian could not stand.

Ethan's heart skipped a beat as Sebastian's body went still in his arms. Panic flooded his senses, overwhelming him like a crashing wave. His hands shook as he gently laid Sebastian down, his heart racing with fear. Everything seemed to blur as shock and confusion engulfed his mind, leaving him struggling to make sense of what had just happened.

Tears welled in Ethan's eyes as he realized that Sebastian had stopped breathing and his eyelids did not move. He looked around swiftly to see if someone would come to help him, but no one was around. A deep sense of helplessness and sadness washed over him.

He thought to himself, "Why send me here if the plan was to take his life away? Why is all of this happening around me?" His tears rolled down his face as he closed Sebastian's eyes with his hands.

Amid the chaos of emotions, he found a small comfort in knowing that Sebastian had passed peacefully, believing he was reuniting with his beloved wife.

While wiping away his tears, Ethan felt a tap on his shoulder. Turning around, he saw a man with teary eyes. The man, supporting Ethan to stand up on his legs, gestured with his hands, indicating he wanted something. Initially confused, Ethan understood when the man pointed to the water bottle that he was asking for the empty bottle.

After returning the empty water bottles, Ethan stood there clueless. Four others approached him, tears in their eyes, signaling him to step aside from Sebastian's body. They carried Sebastian away.

Once they left, Ethan glanced at the chocolate and the white rose on the ground. Leaving the park, he pondered these strange events without answers. Why did his professor give him the chocolate and rose? How did the old man know he would bring them? Why could only the old man talk to him? How did the people who came after Sebastian's death know he would be dead?

Lost in thought and grief, Ethan headed back home. The street was empty and quiet. Parking his bicycle, he entered his house to find his parents at the dining table, hands raised for lunch. They smiled and gestured for him to join, but Ethan was not hungry. His parents' expressions did not change.

Feeling uneasy and with unanswered questions, Ethan went to his room to rest. After a while, he decided to take a bath to refresh himself. Dressed and refreshed, he went downstairs for lunch, finding his parents in the same position. They smiled, and as he started eating, his parents dropped their hands and began eating too.

After having lunch, Ethan went to his room and looked out the window. The town was still, and he could hear the wind gently rustling the trees. The Sun was high, and it seemed like everyone was resting indoors.

Sitting on his bed, Ethan wondered if these unusual happenings were the work of God. He questioned why he seemed to act independently while others appeared controlled. The raised hands puzzled him. Was God favoring or disliking him?

In the evening, when people emerged from their houses, Ethan stayed in his room, unsure of what to do. While contemplating the strange events, a gentle wind whispered "Smile" through his window. Surprised, he looked around but found no one. Glancing at the list he had made for his life goals, Lily came to mind.

Excited, Ethan wanted to learn more about Lily amid the mysterious occurrences. Uncertain about how long this situation would last, he felt the urge to search for Lily immediately.

Ethan rushed out of his house and realized his bicycle was missing. He felt a mix of sadness and excitement, thinking it might have been taken by someone normal. In a moment, a boy approached him with the bicycle. Though Ethan had seen the boy around in his neighborhood, they had never spoken. The boy, about Ethan's age, handed him the bicycle, smiled, tapped his shoulder, and left.

Perplexed, Ethan wondered why the boy borrowed his bicycle and returned it just when he needed it. It seemed more than a coincidence, leading Ethan to believe he needed to find Lily's house.

Determined to see the loveliest smile in town, Ethan rode fast, fueled by the thought of seeing Lily's smile. He roughly knew where her house was on the other side of town and had an advantage in knowing Lily's mother and her car.

Ethan reached the part of town where he planned to search for Lily's house. Excitedly, he checked all the houses on the street, but could not find it. Despite feeling upset, he refused to give up. Calming himself down, he began a more thorough search without rushing.

After a few houses, he noticed Lily's mother's black sedan parked in front of a big beautiful house. In his initial excitement, he had missed it.

Reflecting on the experience, Ethan realized the importance of staying calm. Thanking the universe for its grateful lesson, he entered the house through the large gates. Inside, he felt a welcoming atmosphere, with a pleasant breeze, and a sweet scent. Hoping to find

Lily, he called out her name but received no response. Undeterred, he started searching the house which contained four master bedrooms and several smaller rooms.

Knowing Lily's father would likely be outside, Ethan focused on finding Lily's mother. After checking the first two master bedrooms without success, he entered the third, which seemed to be in use. The room was filled with materials related to the human body—pictures illustrating the anatomy of the brain, heart, and other organs adorned the walls, and scattered books suggested research on the human body was being conducted.

Suddenly, Ethan heard footsteps and looked towards the room's entrance. Lily's mother appeared, raising her hands. For a moment, Ethan felt a bit uneasy, but relief washed over him when she smiled. Awkwardly, he tried to express himself, using random words that did not make much sense. They were all half-words used as fillers for a sentence of weird sounds. Realizing Lily's mother probably knew why he was there, he decided not to explain.

Lily's mother gestured for Ethan to follow her, leading him to the main living hall and offering him some fruit snacks. As Ethan enjoyed the snacks, he eagerly anticipated seeing Lily. However, after waiting for about an hour, Lily did not appear.

As darkness set in, Ethan started feeling doubtful about meeting Lily. Suddenly, he heard footsteps and hoped it was Lily, but it turned out to be Lily's father, carrying gardening tools. Unlike Lily's mother, he did not smile, and his facial features were mostly hidden by a bushy mustache and beard. Fearing a misunderstanding, Ethan nervously babbled words until he saw Lily's father smile, calming his nerves. It took a few deep breaths for Ethan to return to normal after Lily's father went inside the house.

Ethan sat back on the couch, hoping to see Lily soon. Meanwhile, Lily's parents began doing household chores and later went into the kitchen to cook. Suddenly, the house became silent, making Ethan curious about what was happening. Worried that everyone might have turned into statues, he hurried to the kitchen only to find Lily's parents sharing a kiss. Witnessing the moment, Ethan smiled to himself and returned to the couch. Eventually, the usual sounds of kitchen activities resumed.

As the night approached, Ethan started losing hope of seeing Lily that day and wondered where she might have gone. Feeling the need to return home for dinner, he decided to leave Lily's house with a heavy heart.

Before riding his bicycle home, he looked up at the sky, raised his hands, and expressed his confusion and frustration, "Why are you giving me false hopes? Why am I here?"

Riding towards home, he reached his room and felt sad about not being able to see Lily. The thought that the universe might not want them to be together made him emotional, and tears rolled down his face as he lay on his bed.

Feeling sad for a while, Ethan remembered it was time for dinner. He did not wish for his emotions to affect his parents. He went downstairs, and his parents were waiting for him, just like during breakfast, and lunch.

Despite his efforts, Ethan found it hard to eat, feeling pain in his lower throat while swallowing his food. Tears rolled down his cheeks and into his mouth, and he felt the salty taste of tears mixing with his food. His parents, too, were in tears, struggling to eat.

Realizing that his sadness might be affecting his parents, Ethan tried to overcome it. He shifted his focus away from the thoughts about Lily and concentrated on happy memories with his parents. Recalling a special moment that he considered one of the happiest in his life, he managed to overcome his sadness, at least temporarily. Shifting his thoughts required a lot of mental effort, but he saw a positive change in his parents' expressions. Wiping away their tears, they moved past the moment of sadness.

After dinner, Ethan went to his room upstairs, sat on his chair, and looked out the window at the night sky. The familiar sounds of insects filled the night air.

Suddenly, he realized something was missing, the birds. He could not recall seeing any birds throughout the day, not even at the crow's nest. As he replayed the events of his day in his mind, he realized he had not seen any animals, including pet dogs, and cats on the streets.

Chapter 3

Normal is Hard to Find

The next day morning, Ethan was still unable to hear any birds. He opened the window and saw the Sun was about to rise. Things did not turn back to normal. Looking out the window, he could see his neighbors meditating. All of them, whom he had never seen wake up early, were sitting on the floor with their eyes closed, focusing on their breathing, with their hands resting on their thighs, palm facing up, with the fingers relaxed. Except for one, a small boy, who was chaotically walking on the street with his hands raised. He moved away from the window just when he realized that the boy's movements did not seem to be controlled. He returned to look through the window but could not find the boy.

He could have joined the others to meditate or could have gone in search of the boy to clarify his doubt, but his heart, and mind were not willing to. He did his daily chores and went downstairs to see his parents just wrapping up their meditation and stretching their muscles. His parents still had their hands raised.

He was sitting on the couch in his living room not knowing what to do that day. He lost the belief that he would be able to find someone normal like him. He did not have the nerve to visit Lily's house as he was already recovering from the events of the previous night, especially because he thought that the universe did not want them to end up together. This thought appeared in his mind because the universe did not even let him look at Lily's smile again.

His breakfast was ready. But today he did not want his mother to get up from her chair during her breakfast to get a glass of water for him. As soon as he emptied the glass of water, he went to the kitchen to fetch water.

After breakfast, he went to his room to think about what he could be doing that day. His deep thought was distracted by a sound. It was a familiar sound and he had heard it every day except the previous day. It was the barking of a dog.

He heard it at a distance, and he immediately peeked out of his window to look for the dog. Except it was not one dog, but many! The dogs were all being taken for a walk on the street by their owners.

The dogs were acting a bit unusual. It seemed like they were distracted for a moment, then kept trying to listen to something in constant intervals and then moving forward. It appeared as though someone gave them instructions about what needed to be done and where they needed to go, but were unable to control them for an extended period. The human owners held onto the harness, just in case the dogs did not listen and went wild.

Ethan ran downstairs and noticed a couple of bicycles parked in front of each house. Beside his bicycle, he saw another one parked. He did not know to whom the bicycle belonged, but it was not new. It looked like it was years old. Not only were there bicycles, but in front of some houses, he saw human-operable rickshaws and skateboards. He simply noticed that none of the vehicles had an engine and had to be operated with the help of humans. Everything needed to be physically driven by humans with their physical movement.

Ethan stood there wondering what all this was about. He wondered if God was doing this because he had heard his prayers about saving the environment, to make a better, and cleaner world for the next generations to come.

He shifted his focus onto the dogs and noticed that it was not only dogs but all other pets as well. Pet cats were being carried by the owners themselves in their arms. Pet birds were still being carried in their cages. People who had many pets were carrying only one or two of their pets and the others were being carried by their neighbors who were not owning a pet.

All the caged pet animals and birds were being gathered at a point at the end of each street. The pets were being loaded into several pushing carts.

The carts were being loaded with caged animals and birds, in a way to make sure that the pets did not hurt each other. Ethan noticed that the pets in his neighborhood that had separation anxiety and could not stay calm while being away from their owners, were being carried in their owners' arms instead of being loaded into the cart. This would help them keep their pets relaxed. Each cart was being gently pulled by a person making sure the pets were not traumatized further.

All the people, including Ethan's father, began to walk in a particular direction. Thomas took the bicycle that was parked beside Ethan's bicycle, along with another bicycle that was in their neighbor's house. Instead of riding, his father walked between the two bicycles, pushing them forward. He noticed a similar pattern among others as well. Some were carrying two skateboards in their hands.

Ethan was curious to know where everyone was heading with their pets. He took his bicycle and began following them. They walked for nearly two hours and reached their neighboring town, Koodam. People from that town were all waiting with their hands raised. They all greeted the people from Ethan's town. The pet owners then distributed each of their pets to everyone in that town and returned to their homes.

Ethan understood the reason for people carrying two skateboards and pushing two bicycles instead of riding them. It was for the person carrying the pets and walking with the pets to return to their homes faster. But the only thing that Ethan was not sure about was the reason why every pet from their town was being transferred to this neighboring town.

Suddenly a person collided with Ethan's arm while Ethan was simply standing in the middle of the busy street. Ethan turned to look at that person, but he could not properly see that person's face. He figured it was a girl and seemed like she was moving in a hurry.

Ethan did not realize soon enough that the person was moving in a rush without her hands being raised. Ethan had not seen anyone in a hurry the previous day.

He realized that she could be normal and quickly skimmed through the crowd of people walking across the street. He found the girl at a distance and began moving towards her. He could not run initially as there were people in between, but soon the people stood aside to make way for him. It gave him an advantage to run and catch up with the girl faster.

He followed her for a while but she suddenly disappeared into the crowd. He could not find her as the crowd with their hands raised was easily blocking his vision. He thought he could get into a taller building to look around which could give him an advantage in searching for the girl. He looked around for a taller building and to his surprise, saw the girl he was looking for, peeking through a building's window.

She did not have her hands raised, but looked tense, and was searching for something.

Ethan felt happy to realize that he had found someone who was normal. The girl looked worried. Ethan could know that from her sad facial reactions and the way she was mouthing some words and looking around eagerly. In her search, she did not notice Ethan standing among the people walking with their hands raised. But Ethan could see her face.

He felt goosebumps on his hands and head as the girl strongly resembled his long-lost, presumed-deceased sister. His mind told him that she was not his sister, but his heart felt that she was.

His eyes filled with tears as he said, "Emily!"

He ran towards the building and went upstairs. The girl was still looking out the window. She turned to look at Ethan as she heard his footsteps. Ethan was very happy and tears of happiness began flowing from his eyes as he saw his sister standing in front of him. Words struggled to come out of his mouth. The girl too, seemed happy to see him, a normal person. But with no time to express her happiness, she asked for help to search for a boy in the crowd with short blond hair who also was normal.

Ethan did not have time to think about anything at that moment other than to search for that boy his sister was looking for. He peeked out of the window to see if he could see anyone with the identification his sister had mentioned. He thought that it would be a waste of time if they were both looking through the same window. So, he decided to go to the terrace of the building to look for that boy. But they could not find that boy with the short blond hair.

He returned to his sister, who was sitting on the floor, weeping. Ethan tried consoling her, but she did not seem to be hearing Ethan's words. Ethan felt that she might not have recognized him, but he did not want to ask her about his doubts at that time. His sister could not stop crying. Ethan sat on the stairs wondering what he could be doing to calm his sister down.

After a while, two girls about the same age as his sister came upstairs. One of them was carrying a red, thin cloth made of cotton and the other was carrying a small brown colored puppy.

Ethan made way for them to walk up the stairs and they went to his sister. They handed the puppy and the red cloth to her and made her stand up. They hugged her to console her. They began humming a melody that seemed to have made his sister better.

When his sister stopped crying and focused on taking care of the puppy, the two girls left with their hands raised.

She looked at Ethan and said, "It is good to see a person who is able to speak. My name is Anabelle."

Ethan was shocked to hear her say her name was Anabelle. He became emotional, unable to process that she could not be his sister. He asked, "Anabelle? But…" How could this be possible, he thought.

He found it difficult to talk as he was controlling himself not to cry. Anabelle saw the struggle in Ethan and asked him if he was alright. Ethan was unable to answer her question. She thought that it was due to her recent crying and broken state that was making Ethan feel sad.

She said, "Oh, please don't mind my crying. Somehow deep down I felt that this would happen to me one day. I just did not expect that it would be this quick. But I am very happy that the universe did not leave me to handle it by myself. I thank the universe for sending you here. It is good to have someone to talk to when you are in pain. Oh, sorry! I have been talking about myself for a while. I forgot to ask your name."

Ethan struggled but managed to say his name out loud and then he asked, "Do you not remember me?"

Anabelle looked at Ethan and tried to recollect if she had seen him anywhere. But as she could not, she answered, "No."

Ethan asked her if she could show her right elbow. Anabelle wondered why he asked her to show him her elbow, as she showed her elbow to him.

Ethan looked at her elbow and with tears in his eyes, he said, "You are my sister, Emily. I remember the scar very well. I still remember the day you got that scar. You fell on a rock while I was chasing you when we were young. The same scar, in the same place. I can surely say that you are my sister. My sister, the river wanted to make part of itself when she was five years old. My sister whom we assumed to be dead though we could not find the body. But somehow deep in my heart, I knew that you were still alive."

Anabelle said, "You must have mistaken me for someone else, Ethan. My name is not Emily, it is Anabelle. And I surely did not get this scar from falling on rocks. I got this when I was ten years old. I fell unconscious as I ran into a tree when I was being chased by a group of dogs. That is how I got this scar."

Ethan could not believe his eyes and ears. He said, "How can there be another girl in this world who looks exactly like my mother when she was in her twenties, has my father's eyes, and has the same scar as my sister? And she too would have been your age now if she had not drowned!"

Ethan further began asking about her childhood. From what Anabelle said, Ethan figured that she was from that part of the town to which the pets were being given and had never been outside of that town. He wanted to know more about her family, so he asked her if he could meet them one day.

Anabelle said, "Yeah sure. I do not have much to do today. Frankly, I do not know what to do today. I had some places to visit with Marcus. But as he is gone, I am not sure I can visit that place all by myself. It wouldn't make sense. There is nothing interesting for me to do today. So, if you are free, we can visit my family today. At least I will have someone to talk to for the rest of my day."

Ethan immediately accepted her invitation and they went to Anabelle's house. Meanwhile, some of the people from Ethan's town began returning to their town after leaving their pets in that town. Ethan wanted to show Emily to his father but he was nowhere to be seen.

They both looked around to see the people of Anabelle's town taking care of the pets of Ethan's town. They both wondered about the possible reason for the transfer of the pets from one town to another.

As they walked towards Anabelle's house, Ethan asked worriedly, "What do you think is happening around us?"

Anabelle admitted, "I have no clue, but it's really scary."

Ethan pondered, "I'm curious why only the pets are being moved from Mandrook to Koodam."

Anabelle said, "I hope nothing worse happens. I can't handle too much sadness all at once."

Ethan said, "I feel the same way."

Anabelle inquired, "Are you the only normal person from your town?"

Ethan nodded sadly, replying, "Yeah, it's been pretty lonely."

Anabelle sympathetically responded, "That must have been really hard for you. At least I had Marcus beside me."

Ethan enquired about the boy with the short blond hair. He wanted to know about Marcus as he was normal, but ultimately, he wanted to know about the person his sister's heart had bonded with love. Asking about him made her sad, but she managed to tell him about Marcus.

Anabelle said, "Marcus and I met last year in my college. We felt a deep connection between us. I can't explain the connection. It was like magic.

But as time passed, he was not acting like his actual self. He often did not remember what he was doing. He just woke up from his sleep and wandered around the streets at night.

When everyone began walking with their hands raised, he said he was hearing a voice and claimed that it was calling him to do evil things. He also disclosed that he had been hearing voices in his head for a long time. Usually, they were soft and soothing, but this time he said it was a different voice—forceful and angrier.

Up until last night, we checked every house in Koodam, but we didn't find anyone acting normally. We decided to visit Mandrook to see if its people also had their hands raised. It was almost midnight when we were heading to your town. A mysterious light guided us and we stumbled upon a place where we witnessed something marvelous. Words cannot describe it. It was an experience that can only be truly understood by seeing it for yourself.

At that spot, he seemed greatly disturbed. He began dancing strangely, and fear gripped me as I watched his ferocious movements. His face was contorted with anger, his eyes blazing with fury. It was an intensity of emotion that I had never seen in him before. After a while, the ferocity of his dance began to subside, and he transitioned into a slower, more graceful rhythm. His expression softened, and his eyes regained their familiar warmth. The latter part of his dance was a thing of beauty to watch.

I attempted to speak to him, but it was as if he couldn't hear me. It was as though I were invisible to him. I stood there, feeling utterly helpless, unsure of what to do next.

Suddenly, his anger peaked, and he began his ferocious dance. And then he collapsed to the ground, unable to bear the pain in his head. He was fighting against the voice. It was agonizing to watch him twitch on the ground. The only help I could offer was to carry him away from that place. I brought him back to our town where he found some relief and the voice began to diminish. He slept through the night, but I couldn't. I dozed off for a bit early in the morning. When I woke up, he was gone, and the people from your town started visiting ours with their pets."

On seeing his sister cry, the brother in Ethan, whom he had forgotten, wanted to express his support in the most amazing way possible. He wanted to take all the problems from her life and carry them on his shoulders. But as he was not an expressive person, he just said, "Things will get better."

When they were just about to enter Anabelle's house, they heard a loud noise. It was from the direction of Ethan's town. Also, it was where Anabelle had seen Marcus head. Both of them knew that it was not a usual sound. They knew that it had come from quite a distance. The sound was not the only unusual thing that was happening. All the people around stopped for a second and their facial reactions showed that they were all in shock.

The shock among the people did not last for very long. After five seconds they all went back to their state as before. Anabelle did not find the people's shock out of context considering their recent behavior. She was more focused on the sound and was thinking if Marcus had something to do with it. Ethan had not seen such a change in reaction among the people. Whatever happened the previous day and till that moment was predicted and the actions were already in place. So, the change in the reaction among the people caused a question in Ethan's mind.

If all the people were under the control of someone who knows and controls everything, then could the shock among the people mean that someone or something is acting without the knowledge of the one in control?

At that time, it did not seem to be important to visit Anabelle's parents. It felt important to investigate the sound. What or who could have caused it?

Ethan and Anabelle got on their bicycles and began riding in the direction from where the sound came from. They traveled for a long time but could not find any clue about the source of the sound. On their way, Anabelle showed him a big tree, standing alone in an open field. She pointed to the north of the lone tree and said that the place where Marcus did his weird dance was just a few meters from that tree.

Ethan began to wonder if the marvelous place his sister mentioned could be connected to the strange sound. He was on the verge of asking his sister to take him to the spot where Marcus had danced, but his thoughts were interrupted by the ringing of a bicycle bell.

They saw a person ringing his bicycle bell and beckoning them to follow him on his way towards Ethan's town. This person happened to be the last one returning to Mandrook after leaving his pet at Anabelle's town. Hoping that following this person would help them unravel the mystery of the sound, they decided to accompany him. However, their search yielded no clues about the source of the sound. They simply followed the person back to Mandrook.

Ethan thought that the reason the man asked them to follow him to his town could be because the one in control wanted his sister to return to her parents.

As they were already in Mandrook, he thought of bringing his sister back to his home. As it was already time for lunch, he insisted, "Emily, would you allow me to take out one single problem from your mind?"

Anabelle asked, "Is it about you referring to me as Emily?"

Ethan thought in his mind, "You are Emily. You just have forgotten that bit." But he did not say it out loud as he was tired and hungry and did not want to argue about it. So instead, he said, "No. I was talking about food. The Sun is at its peak. I am already very tired. Shall we go home for lunch?"

Anabelle initially hesitated, but she could not avoid the kind invitation from Ethan. So, she decided to go with him.

Ethan said, "I am just wondering if your parents are aware of you having lunch at my home. I do not want them to be waiting for your arrival."

Anabelle said, "I don't think that would be a problem. I am sure they would not be worried if I did not show up for lunch because they know that I would be safe. They raised me as an independent girl and know I can handle things on my own. I am fine with eating my leftover lunch for dinner if my family has prepared it. I do not like wasting food."

Ethan felt that Anabelle had misunderstood the context of his question. So, he asked for reassurance, "I just did not want your parents to wait for your arrival to eat their lunch. Something similar happened here yesterday."

Anabelle asked, "Yesterday? Why? What happened yesterday?"

Ethan said, "Yesterday my parents waited for me to eat the food before they began. Didn't it happen to you?"

Anabelle responded, "Really? I didn't notice that. I had been in shock all day, mostly searching the town with Marcus. So, I might have missed it."

Ethan reflected, "I guess we probably shouldn't worry too much about it. Especially with everything that's been happening lately and people being aware of what's coming next, I hope they're already aware of this change of plans by now."

Both Anabelle and Ethan arrived at Ethan's house. As expected, Ethan's parents seemed to know about Anabelle's arrival and they welcomed Anabelle with a tight hug. Their faces were filled with happiness with tears of happiness flowing from his mother's eyes as she kissed Anabelle on her forehead. These gestures made Anabelle wonder if she really was Emily. But deep down, she could not accept that she was Emily. Ethan was certain that Anabelle was Emily, but he hesitated to impose the truth on his sister as he feared that forcing the truth on her might cause her to reject it. So he decided to give it some time.

Everyone settled to have lunch, but his parents were waiting for Emily to begin her meal. While eating, Ethan's mother had tears in her eyes. Ethan thought that some dust might have fallen into his mother's eyes. But Anabelle felt there was something more to the tears.

After lunch, Anabelle asked Ethan, "You called me Emily when you saw me for the first time. Does she look like me?"

Ethan was about to explain to her that she was Emily. But he felt that Anabelle might not be ready to accept the fact that she is Emily. So, he said, "As I told you. The possibility of two people looking alike, with the same age, and the same scar is very rare. So I consider you as my sister, Emily, and it's not going to change until someone proves that you are not my sister."

Anabelle said, "I could see it in your parents' eyes. They see me as their daughter. I am so sorry for your sister. If she is still alive, I hope she will be reunited with your family soon."

Ethan thought to himself, "She is and she has already been reunited with her family and I am looking at her."

Ethan's parents left the two of them and retired to their room to rest. Ethan and Emily found themselves restricted from leaving the house. Every time they attempted to step outside, someone seemingly appeared out of nowhere to obstruct their path. These people stood in front of them, blocking their path. Ethan tried various tactics to get past them, like jumping, rolling, and crawling, but nothing worked. He was determined to leave, but then three people showed up at their door, blocking their way out.

Recognizing the futility of their attempts, they resigned themselves to rest, putting their trust in whoever was in control. They remained indoors, hoping that the source of the sound was being addressed. They wondered why they were being blocked from leaving their house.

Ethan shared his thoughts about the sound and his opinion about people's shock. Anabelle shared her opinion that the sound could be related to Marcus.

Yet they were not sure about why the pets were all transferred from Ethan's town to another. What could be the goal? Why are people in this state? And why were only Ethan, Anabelle, and Marcus? Could Marcus be controlled by someone other than the one who is controlling everyone? Is it a fight between two higher-dimension beings? A lot of questions, but none had an answer.

In the evening, Ethan asked Emily, "Do you have to go?"

He wished for his sister to stay but she insisted on returning to her house.

Anabelle said, "I understand that you think of me as Emily and you want me to stay with your family. But I need to get back to my family. They need me, especially in this situation. I still do not have any idea about the things happening around me. So please do not stop me."

Ethan asked, "At least, can I accompany you today to see the marvelous thing you saw at the place where Marcus danced weirdly?"

Anabelle was not ready to visit that marvelousness, especially after what she had seen it do to Marcus. So, she politely refused.

She said, "Oh. The marvelous thing happens only at midnight. But as I lost my sleep last night, I don't think I can make it today. I need to sleep to be able to walk tomorrow. And the bicycle ride to your place intensified my tiredness. Maybe tomorrow we can visit it if you are fine with it."

Ethan was aware of what sleeplessness does to a person's mental and physical health. Considering his sister's well-being, he agreed with her. He was not planning on visiting the place alone that day as he thought he might not know what to look for.

Lost in thoughts about the mysterious sound and the enchanting place, he forgot to accompany his sister back to her town. He was confident that nothing bad would befall his sister, and even if it did, help would swiftly come her way.

As Anabelle was about to leave, Ethan along with his parents waved their hands and wished her a safe ride back.

Ethan knew that the next day was going to be really long. So, he went to bed earlier, happy with the thought that he found his sister.

Chapter 4

The Trail of Flowers and the Colossal Beast

The next morning, just before Ethan woke up, he had a dream. It was the same dream he had two nights ago when everything started. He thought it was important, so he tried to focus on the small details in his dream.

He sat upright on his bed and thought to himself, "Why am I having the same dream again? How could this be possible? If it had happened a week ago, I might have been in shock. But now, this is not even shocking to me."

A lion's loud roar echoed in his room, interrupted his concentration.

The lion's roar made Ethan forget his dream, and it gave him chills. He looked through his window and saw a lion pride. A majestic male led the group, with four lionesses, and six cubs following behind, each a different size.

In the distance, Ethan heard the sounds of elephants and other creatures. The town bustled with the vibrant presence of wildlife that seemed to have come from the forests beyond the Nerupunila towards the west of the twin towns. Ethan couldn't help but ponder how these animals had breached the formidable barrier of the Nerupunila mountain range, which had long served as a natural shield between the towns and the wilderness. The towering peaks of Nerupunila had always provided a sense of safety, keeping the untamed wilderness at bay and ensuring the tranquillity of the townsfolk.

Worried about Emily, Ethan quickly went downstairs to get his bicycle, determined to keep her safe. In his hurry, he briefly forgot the danger of stepping outside, where only bones would be left behind.

A tragic death occurrence from the mouths of the lion pride was avoided in this story by Ethan's father.

As Ethan hurried down the stairs toward the main door, he found Thomas blocking his way. It struck him that his father was intentionally keeping him from leaving his own home. A sense of calm came over him, knowing that his sister was likely being protected with the same care. He had faith that she would be safe.

Ethan's father, taking on the role of a guardian, stood firmly by the door, preventing Ethan from leaving the house. Throughout the day, there was a chaotic movement of groups of animals migrating from the west to the east. Ethan guessed that this migration might be the reason why pets were relocated to another town the previous day; to avoid any harm to the pets from the wild animals.

On the third day of the people walking with their hands raised, activities were subdued, with the entire day dedicated to the careful transfer of wild animals. Everyone chose to stay indoors to prevent loss of life and ensure peaceful travel for the wild animals.

But why and where were they headed?

Ethan took the opportunity to observe various animals and become familiar with their distinct sounds. Many of these sounds were entirely new to him, making him realize that his mental images were quite different from the reality of these sounds.

The carnivorous animals were the first to cross the town, followed by the omnivores. As the afternoon progressed, the number of animals crossing diminished. From evening until nightfall, it was the herbivores. Concerned about encountering wild animals during midnight wanderings, Ethan decided not to visit the marvelous place that night, prioritizing caution.

The next day, he hopped on his bicycle and headed toward Emily's house. Moving with great care, he kept a watchful eye for any signs of wild animals. His cautious approach led to an unusual discovery as he neared the spot where the marvelous event had occurred.

A sense of unease washed over him as he approached the area. He saw a few eagles flying around. Exercising caution, he stopped his bicycle on the road near the lone tree. The tree brought back memories of his sister describing Marcus's peculiar dance near that spot.

Curiosity propelled him toward the eagles. He wondered what they could be eating, as it was the first bird he had seen in three days. He hoped he would not encounter any wild beasts along the way.

His shock deepened when he saw a massive animal lying lifeless, its flesh mostly consumed. The flesh around the head was entirely gone, leaving behind a skull larger than that of two elephants combined. Watching vultures devour the remaining flesh, he wondered about the identity of the colossal creature they were feasting on.

Where did it come from? What could have consumed its flesh so quickly, leaving only scant remains for the vultures and eagles?

He noticed some trees around the creature showing signs of scorching, and the ground below had ash sediment. Fear took hold of him. He wondered if an even larger creature might be responsible for burning the creature to death. He thought the fire might explain why there was so little flesh left on the creature.

Backing away, he murmured, "Could it be Kargoor?"

He pedaled vigorously to his sister's house, unaware of the shock awaiting him. A shock that turned out to be very unpleasant. Upon arriving at his sister's house, he saw the door open. Inside, he saw two people sitting on the couch with hands raised, tears in their eyes.

Ethan realized they were Emily's foster parents, and their distressed expressions worried him. He searched the house but found no sign of Emily. Anabelle's father handed him a piece of paper with the word "MARVELOUS" written on it. Deeply concerned, he feared for her safety and prayed for her well-being.

Worried that the people and the controller were unaware of his sister's whereabouts, his mind focused on Marcus and the mysterious sound he heard during his last visit to Koodam.

He wondered if there was a connection between his sister's disappearance, Marcus, the dead creature, and the marvelous location. Intent on finding some clues, he headed to the marvelous place.

Approaching the marvelous place, he noticed a cluster of flowers beneath the lone tree. The vivid red blooms caught his eye from afar. As Emily had mentioned to him about Marcus's fierce dance while they saw that tree the previous day, the red petals stirred his creative imagination, envisioning a person's fierce dance at midnight under the tree. Lost in thoughts of Marcus's dance and the emotions his sister might have experienced, he briefly forgot about the nearby dead colossal creature.

As he reached for the flowers on the roadside, he found red petals followed by a trail of petals in different colors. The floral path led toward his town, something he had not noticed earlier that morning. It seemed like the flowers were guiding him somewhere, and driven by curiosity, he followed the floral path.

The path led him to the heart of his town, where he found a beverage shop. Inside, everyone was walking around with their hands raised, enjoying slices of fresh fruit in a serene atmosphere. Eager to understand why he was guided there, he looked around, momentarily captivated by the shop owner expertly slicing a juicy red fruit.

The juice splashed as the big fruit got sliced, making him instantly thirsty. The craving for a delicious bite of the juicy, red fruit with black seeds became too tempting. At that moment, his mind blanked out, and he couldn't think of anything else as he moved towards the alluring fruit.

Without saying a word, the shop owner gave him a bowl filled with expertly sliced watermelon. Gratefully accepting the refreshing treat, he thanked the shopkeeper, saying it was exactly what he needed. Sitting at a nearby table, he looked forward to the burst of juicy flavor on his taste buds.

As he was about to bite into a carefully cut triangular watermelon piece, an unexpected event grabbed his attention. A gentle touch on his shoulder startled him, and he quickly turned to see who it was. He was hoping to see Emily, but it was not her. At that moment, his thirst seemed to disappear, and he was frozen, captivated by the enchanting sight of Lily's smile.

Lily said Ethan's name with a questioning tone, standing behind him. The shop owner offered her a bowl of sliced pineapple, and Lily gracefully took a seat across from Ethan. Still in disbelief, Ethan held the watermelon, mouth hanging open.

Seeing his surprised expression, Lily asked, "Aren't you going to eat that?"

Ethan replied, "No… (stuttered) I mean… (awkward smile) Yes. I am going to eat it."

Lily's expression turned serious as she said, "You better hurry up. We must understand what's happening before our life ends."

Ethan's eyes widened, and he asked, "Life ends?"

Lily explained, "Yeah. Did you see any birds or insects after people started walking with their hands raised? Imagine a world without bees. Our lands would become barren without them, which means no food. Without food, our lives would be at stake."

Ethan said, "I saw some birds today."

Lily urgently stood up and responded, "What? Take me to the location right away."

Ethan nodded and said, "Sure. I'll take you there, but let's enjoy these fruit bowls first. They were given to us with love, and it wouldn't be right to waste them. Besides, there's no need to rush. The birds aren't going anywhere. I'm sure they still have two day's work ahead of them."

He took a bite of the watermelon in his hand, the sweetness filled his mouth. He wanted to offer a piece from his bowl to Lily. However, doubt crept in, eroding his confidence. They exchanged glances, and Lily awaited Ethan's next words. As Ethan contemplated Lily's potential reactions, the silence grew awkward. Trying to break it, he asked, "How did you end up here?"

Lily relaxed and shared, "I was reading at the library, totally into the subject. Suddenly, someone came to me out of nowhere and pointed in a direction. That person did not seem to give up until I walked in that direction, so I followed the guidance. Outside the library, another person directed me further. Following the directions led me to this shop. I saw someone walking normally without their hands raised, which surprised me. I hesitated to enter the shop, fearing it might be something dangerous. But then, it felt familiar, like I had seen that person before. When I saw your face, Ethan, I felt relieved."

Ethan felt excited as Lily talked to him. It felt like his dreams were coming true, a cosmic nudge to kiss her. While Lily spoke, a silent battle raged in Ethan's mind. He debated whether to lean in for a kiss or not, but he realized it was too soon. Fear stopped him from making a rash decision that could have consequences. Taking the time to think prevented a potential misstep in their budding connection.

After finishing their fruit bowls, they thanked the shop owner for the bowls and reached the spot where Ethan had first seen the lifeless creature. Lily, on seeing the skull of the colossal beast, said, "Now, my fear about the end of our life has increased."

Ethan added, "When I saw it this morning, there was enough food for vultures and eagles for two days. I never thought that in this short time, the birds would eat all the flesh and leave only the bones."

Lily asked, "What do you think this is? And what could have killed this creature?"

Ethan replied, "I have no idea. But this place has a certain mystery. My sister mentioned seeing something amazing somewhere near here that only happens at night."

Lily said, "Wait, you have a sister? I thought you were the only child to your parents."

Ethan questioned, "You know that much about me?"

Lily answered, "Yeah, you're my classmate, and your parents and mine were friends."

Ethan astonishingly asked, "You know about that too?"

Lily explained, "Yeah, I remember the argument they had. I was there then and so were you."

Ethan shared, "Was I present when they argued? I am unable to recollect anything about it. I found out about this only a few days ago."

Lily redirected, "Okay, let's not lose track. You were talking about your sister."

Ethan started, "Oh yeah. Long story short, I had a sister who we thought was dead," briefly explaining about his sister, her unique scar, and Marcus.

Lily said, "Well, that's a lot to take in. Where is she?"

Ethan's worry surfaced as he explained, "I don't know. That's why I'm concerned. I couldn't find her in her house. My search for her led me here. I followed the trail of flowers, hoping it would lead me to her, which led me to that shop where you found me. But I still haven't found my sister. I believe this creature and the marvelous event could hold the answer to finding her."

Lily offered assurance, "I know the place where we can begin our search."

Lily guided Ethan back to their town, leading him to the familiar surroundings of the town's library. Her confidence in navigating the shelves and finding the sections about ancient mystery creatures and stories was clear. With purposeful strides, she selected a couple of books and arranged them neatly on a table. Together, they delved into the pages, scanning through the texts to find information about the mysterious deceased creature.

Perplexed, Ethan asked, "How do you know where you can find these books? It's as if you've lived here."

Lily smiled and replied, "Not lived. You are referring to it as past tense. But you should be referring to it in the present tense. This has been my new home for the past three days."

Realization dawned on Ethan. This explained why he couldn't find Lily the day he waited for her at her house.

Ethan took a book saying, "What are we going to find in here? Do you hope to find the information about the colossal beasts in here?"

Lily just said, "Hmm… hmm," as she was busy searching for books that could help them.

He was in awe when he read that the world, which he had long thought was flat, was elliptical. Excitedly, he shared this newfound information with Lily, who gave him a judgmental look. Ethan quickly defended himself, saying, "Hey, don't give me that look. I've been living in my grandmother's stories and never considered the possibility of the world not being flat. Guess I might have slept through all the geography classes."

Lily smiled reassuringly and replied, "This explains your low scores in geography all the time. But it's okay. Nobody knows everything. It's nice that you're open to learning something new and willing to accept facts. Many people disagreed and stopped coming to this library, thinking everything there was a lie. But rest assured, this place is a haven of truth. Everything mentioned in the books found here is not falsehood, except for the fiction storybook section that we saw while entering the library."

As they continued to peruse the books, Ethan stumbled upon something crucial. He thought to himself, "I hope the details in this book aren't real and are just a fictional portrayal by an artist, detailing colossal creatures as if they had encountered them in person."

Curious, he turned to Lily and asked, "What do you know about Kargoor?"

Lily furrowed her eyebrows in thought and replied, "Kargoor? Hmm… It doesn't ring a bell. Why do you ask?"

The details in the book reminded him of the stories his grandmother used to tell him when he was young. He shared, "Kargoor is a fire-breathing monster that razed our towns over a thousand years ago. I've heard terrifying tales about it from my grandmother. Our ancestors of the twin towns bound Mandrook and Koodam with magic to keep colossal creatures like Kargoor away from our towns. They built a barrier around our town, making it invisible to the creatures outside and visible only to those with magic running through their bodies."

Lily teased Ethan, saying, "Magical walls protecting our town from fire-breathing monsters and other creatures? Your grandmother must have been quite the storyteller. But it was just a story, wasn't it? Do you believe that these creatures exist? Because if they did, then someone should have seen them, right?"

Ethan replied, "I'm not sure. You told me the world isn't flat but elliptical, right?"

Lily replied doubtfully, "Yeah?"

Ethan continued, "Everything we see around us appears flat, as far as our eyesight reaches. So the only possible explanation for the world to be elliptical is that our towns are just tiny places in a vast world."

Lily, unaware of where Ethan was leading the conversation, replied thoughtfully, "Yeah."

Ethan continued, "I recall numerous occasions where I discussed the wall, magic, and creatures from my grandmother's stories with people. They all reacted the same way—unable to remember the information I had shared with them. They had forgotten the recent conversation I had with them regarding the magic wall and the colossal creatures."

Confused, Lily asked, "I'm not sure I understand where you're going with this."

Ethan explained, "It could mean that the magic wasn't just used on the wall but also on the people of our town."

Lily's eyebrows furrowed as she realized, "So you mean I would forget this conversation we're having about the wall and magic?"

Ethan nodded in agreement, prompting Lily to ask, "But how are you remembering all these things?"

Ethan replied softly, "That's something I'll have to figure out."

Lily paused, observing Ethan, her expression curious as she counted to five in her mind.

Ethan's thoughts wandered as he looked at Lily, looking at him in curiosity, "Wow… Every expression on her face and every action she does makes me want to sweep her up in my arms, fly into the sky, and kiss her. How would it feel if it happened?"

As Lily finished counting, she asked, "When will it happen?"

Ethan briefly entertained the thought that Lily possessed a mysterious ability to read minds, as her question seemed to imply she knew his thoughts about kissing her. Doubtfully, he asked, "What?"

Lily clarified, "I just counted to five, and I still remember our conversation about creatures and magic. How long does it usually take for a person to forget?"

Ethan admitted, "I'm not sure. I didn't keep track of that. Probably like ten minutes maybe."

Lily reassured him, "Oh, okay. If I happen to forget our conversation and disagree with you about the magic, please don't take it personally. I understand how challenging it can be when someone doesn't agree with the facts we present."

Ethan thought to himself, "She cares about me. She's wife material. I want to marry her."

A wave of sadness washed over Ethan as he remembered the beast's skull he had encountered. Dark thoughts clouded his mind, worrying that if the same fate befell his town as the dead beast, there might not be a world for him to love Lily. His concerns were reflected in his expression.

Noticing his troubled demeanor, Lily asked, "What's bothering you?"

Ethan said, "Nothing," as he redirected Lily's attention to a passage in his book, "It talks about a fire-breathing monster that once plagued this world with terror. According to the text, the monster cannot be killed. The passage goes on to describe how various worlds united with magic to safeguard our town, constructing a protective magical barrier around it. This wall acts as our shield, shielding us from the threats of deadly monsters. The book contains information about many such creatures and the protective measures taken."

Lily inquired, "Various worlds united? What is so special about our town that it needs to be protected? What about the whole world? Does this mean that the people in our towns are the only human beings alive on this planet?"

Ethan was traumatized by the number of questions that Lily had asked. He said, "I didn't find answers for most of those in this book. We can search through the other books. But I guess I know the answer to one of the questions. I believe it's me."

Lily curiously asked, "It's you?"

Ethan responded, "Yeah. I am the special thing about this town."

Lily looked at Ethan, expecting him to continue. Ethan, who just wanted to sound cool to get her to like him, thought to himself, "It sounded a lot cooler in my mind. I am an Idiot. I should make her feel special so that she would like me. Not make me special. Think, Ethan! Think twice before you speak. Please, God, help me through this!"

Ethan explained, "I meant to say we. We are the special ones about Mandrook and Koodam. You, Lily, Marcus, and me. Don't you think?"

Curiosity furrowed Lily's eyebrows as she asked, "You probably might be right. But what is special about us? We are just some random people trying to make it through our lives."

Ethan said, "Don't worry. We'll find the answers together. I bet finding the answers would probably be easier than finding the answers for our math problems."

Lily laughed. She looked back at the book at a picture of a black dragon with horns, which reminded her of the skull they had seen earlier. She asked, "Do you think the magic invisible wall is broken?"

Ethan's expression grew serious as he replied, "I wish I could lie about it. But we'll have to check and confirm for ourselves."

Curious, Lily questioned, "Have you ever seen the magic wall?"

Ethan shook his head, "No. I wanted to when I was young, but my parents wouldn't allow it. They said the area beyond the town was dangerous, filled with robbers. And when I got older, math happened. It made me forget all my grandmother's stories and mysteries because solving math equations seemed more mysterious than them."

Concern etched Lily as she queried, "You said there were many monsters described in that book. But why did you ask about Kargoor?"

Ethan explained, "Among the ancient creatures that I have looked through, Kargoor was the only one that could breathe fire. Except for the name and the fact that he could not be killed, there is nothing about him. We might not even recognize him apart from the other colossal beast."

Lily said, "Why would you want to recognize him?" Lily gasped in terror, "You think Kargoor was the one that killed that ginormous creature?"

Ethan somberly nodded, "I am afraid so."

Lily said, "If it's true, both our towns are at stake."

The Sun was at its peak when they stepped out of the library with the book containing information about ancient mystery creatures and a couple of other books that could be useful. Feeling a sense of friendship, Ethan extended an invitation to Lily to join him for lunch at his house. Lily hesitated initially but Ethan insisted that she join him for lunch as it might take time for Lily to reach her home for food. He also said that whoever was in control would have already made his mother prepare food for Lily.

As they strolled toward Ethan's house, Lily pondered aloud, "Ethan, do you believe that whatever is happening is ultimately for the better?"

Ethan nodded thoughtfully, "Yeah, I truly believe so. I have been thinking of ways to improve our town for the next generation. The increase in plastics and industrial waste has taken a toll on our environment. Some have warned that our actions might lead to the end of the world. However, if you consider the history of this planet, we heard from our ancestors, this world has seen many natural disasters and yet managed to regenerate. So, it's not the world that's at risk, but humankind if we do not take serious actions regarding this. That's precisely why I volunteered when you sought help a few days ago. If the entity in control truly wants to end the world, why bother cleaning the streets of our invisible town? Moreover, a couple of other things happened that gave us a positive view of what is happening around us. Maybe the birds and bees were removed from our town for some other purpose and when the purpose is fulfilled, they might return."

Lily sighed, her expression reflecting a mix of sadness and hope, "I hope things improve, and that all of this is happening for the best."

As they arrived at Ethan's house, his parents warmly welcomed them at the doorstep. Ethan's mother, overcome with emotion, embraced Lily tightly, her eyes brimming with tears. Perplexed, Ethan remarked, "The volume of tears from my mother's eyes seems to surpass the amount she shed yesterday upon learning that my sister is alive."

Lily playfully retorted, "Oh, come on. Why would she cry more upon seeing me? Perhaps you didn't observe closely enough yesterday."

Ethan agreed with Lily's observation, and they all gathered around the dining table for lunch. Hungry as ever, Ethan wasted no time in digging into his meal as soon as he took his seat.

During the meal, Lily suddenly remembered that she had left her bicycle unlocked and seized the opportunity to excuse herself to secure it. Ethan, with a mouthful of food, attempted to convey that her bicycle would be safe as people were walking with their hands raised and even if someone borrowed it, they would return it when she needed it. However, his attempt to communicate was hindered by the hearty meal he was enjoying.

Observing that his parents had not started their meal and were patiently waiting, Ethan realized they were not just holding off for him but were also waiting for all the guests to commence. As time passed and Lily didn't return, Ethan decided to wash his hands and check on her.

Stepping outside, he found Lily standing there, looking somewhat confused. Ethan approached Lily and noticed tears streaming down her face. Confused and concerned, he inquired about the reason for her tears. Lily explained that her bicycle was a birthday gift from her mother, and someone had stolen it.

As Ethan surveyed the area where they had parked their bicycles, he discovered that his bicycle was also missing. Attempting to console Lily, he pointed out the absence of his bicycle as well, suggesting that perhaps someone had taken them temporarily but would return them when needed and it would be returned when she wanted it.

Lily, still unsure, decided to trust Ethan when he promised to help find her stolen bicycle. She reluctantly put the matter aside and joined Ethan inside for lunch.

Surprisingly, as Ethan and Lily were about to sit at the dining table, they found that Ethan's parents had already started eating. This made Ethan realize that his parents weren't waiting for the guests to start eating. There was another reason for their mealtime routine. Despite the mystery, Ethan chose to focus on enjoying his food and solving the puzzle of the dead creature, leaving his parents' peculiar dining habits for later.

After lunch, everyone decided to stay indoors. Lily thought about going back to her house for the afternoon and returning in the evening. Although Ethan wanted her to stay, he hesitated to express his feelings. Eventually, he agreed with Lily's suggestion. As Lily left Ethan's house, she was surprised to see a girl her age approaching on Lily's stolen bicycle. Just as Ethan had predicted, the girl gave the bicycle to Lily and left with her hands raised.

Ethan had hoped Lily would stay, but the circumstances didn't seem right for that wish. To his surprise, another girl rushed toward Lily with her hands raised. Ethan watched as the girl approached. The act of running itself was unusual because the planned routine of the past few days had eliminated the need for such haste. Ethan was intrigued by the unexpected turn of events. The girl stopped next to Lily, took the bicycle from her, and quickly rode away. Ethan found himself confused, trying to understand the unfolding situation.

Ethan hurried to Lily, who looked at him and said, "I think I should stay here. Back at my home, there's no one to talk to. If I stay here, we can delve deeper into the investigation of the creatures from the book."

Ethan thought about how Lily's choice to stay might have been influenced by his unspoken request to the universe. However, he wasn't aware of the complete truth behind her decision.

Seated in Ethan's room, they explored the books borrowed from the library, discovering the rich history of their town and ancestors. The texts told a story of a time when various creatures lived peacefully with humans, helping them. However, about a thousand five hundred years ago, something changed, and the creatures turned hostile, attacking humans without a clear reason.

The books left them confused about what had caused this sudden change among the creatures. As they kept reading, a spark of hope emerged. The accounts described a phenomenon called the "Call of Dream," a miraculous event that saved humankind in the town's history. Interestingly, the descriptions of the Call of Dream matched the current behavior observed among the people in their town.

According to the texts, during the Call of Dream, people were influenced by a higher power that sought help from other worlds, using magic to protect their world from hostile creatures. The magical wall surrounding their town, a crucial defense, was built during the last

Call of Dream, lasting for about two hundred and sixteen days.

Interestingly, during this time, individuals had no memory of the events that happened. For most, it felt like they had woken up from a deep sleep to find themselves within the protective walls, safe from the looming threat of creatures. Surprisingly, only a chosen few retained memories of the events, choosing to keep the information secret for the greater good of the people. However, people of the current generation consider the Call of Dream a myth.

Within the volumes, Ethan found a lot of information about special swords, each with unique powers. One sword could summon and control fire, while another could pierce through anything. There was a sword that could control water, one that attracted negative energy, another that governed the forces of air, and yet another that controlled the elements of rock. The last sword was believed to have power over animals.

As Ethan explored the details of these amazing weapons, he got an idea. He imagined using the sword that controlled water and air to clean polluted air and water. He wanted to contribute to creating a healthier and cleaner world for future generations.

Lost in his thoughts about powerful swords, Ethan didn't notice that Lily was upset. When he finally came back to reality, he saw Lily sitting with a heavy heart, on the brink of tears. Worried, he asked her what had happened. Lily, unable to hold back her emotions, began crying. Ethan, unsure of the reason for her tears, felt deeply helpless. Seeing Lily cry for the first time was heartbreaking. To comfort her, he gave her a piece of cloth to wipe her tears and sat next to her, offering a supportive shoulder.

Lily's tears gradually stopped, and she began, "I'm sorry. I couldn't control my emotions. I was thinking about my mom's health condition, and the sadness overwhelmed me." Concerned, Ethan asked, "How serious is it?"

Lily's voice shook as she shared, "It's a heart condition. The doctors have given her about six months to live. I fear that these six months might pass during this Call of Dream period. I might not even get to hear my mother's voice again."

Ethan couldn't believe what he had just heard. Things started to become clear to him—the reason for Lily's mother visiting his parents, the reason why Lily's mother was crying during the visit, and the reason why his mother hugged and cried with Lily that day before lunch.

Ethan didn't want to dig deeper into the topic of Lily's mother, afraid it would bring more tears to her eyes.

Unintentionally, he glanced at the piece of paper his professor gave him on the first day of the Call of Dream.

The message about the belief that things that had happened occurred for good and the ongoing events were unfolding for a good purpose echoed in his mind. However, at that moment, he couldn't fathom what good could come from the pain inflicted upon Lily's mother. He felt a surge of anger directed at the universe, questioning the meaning behind such suffering.

Chapter 5

Sword and Fire

In the evening, Ethan and Lily embarked on a journey to the marvelous place, determined to unravel the mysteries surrounding the peculiar occurrences and the enigmatic creature. Ethan could not shake off the worry that Kargoor might be on the loose, so he remained vigilant, keeping an eye out for any signs. However, their quest for answers had to be momentarily paused as another task awaited completion before they could delve into the heart of the mystery.

As they mounted their bicycles, an unusual phenomenon unfolded—they found themselves being subtly guided, each encounter on the road directing them toward an unknown destination. The road was filled with individuals who seemed to direct them somewhere, using their hands to point them towards a particular direction.

Lily, intrigued between choices, voiced the question, "Should we follow their guidance or stay the course to the marvelous place?"

Ethan paused for a moment, his brows furrowed in deep thought. Ethan said, "It feels as though we're being guided towards something of greater significance than what the marvelous place might reveal."

Lily, intrigued yet cautious, proposed a plan. "I'll head to the marvelous place and explore its mysteries under the cloak of night," she suggested.

While Ethan initially hesitated, the weight of the situation compelled him to agree. He cautioned Lily about the looming threat of Kargoor and implored her to remain vigilant.

Ethan set out on his solitary journey, guided by the directions from those they encountered on the road. The directions led him to a desolate expanse, where the air carried the scent of ash, and an unusual warmth enveloped the surroundings. An unsettling feeling crept into his bones, and an overarching question lingered in his mind – why were the people leading him toward danger?

Ethan's heart raced as he spotted a girl kneeling amid the charred landscape, a haunting reminder of the devastation. At that moment, any reservations he harbored vanished and were replaced by an urgent need to reach the figure. The thought that the girl might be his sister, Emily, and the gravity of the situation eclipsed everything else.

Without hesitation, Ethan sprinted toward her, but Emily, facing the other way, appeared oblivious to his presence. Strangely, she showed no reaction to Ethan's calls, as if caught in a trance. Moving in front of her, Ethan was shocked to find that Emily, though physically present, seemed detached and unresponsive. She struggled to catch her breath, and Ethan's attempts to engage her went unanswered, leaving him bewildered and deeply concerned.

Ethan observed the intensity in Emily's gaze as her eyes bore into an unseen target, locked in fierce determination. In her hands, she wielded a sword with a distinctive mark on its handle—an emblem that stirred a sense of familiarity in Ethan, even though he couldn't quite place where he had encountered it before. The worry etched across Ethan's face deepened as he grappled with the sight of his sister, consumed by an unrelenting rage that left him both perplexed and worried.

Perplexed by the surreal scene unfolding before him, Ethan grappled with the myriad questions swirling in his mind. The presence of the sword in Emily's hands, the charred landscape around them, and the palpable rage in her gaze left him in a state of bewildered shock. The initial flood of inquiries—about the cause of the scorched land and the possibility of Kargoor's involvement—faded into insignificance as Emily collapsed, unconscious.

Desperation gripped Ethan as he attempted to rouse his sister, but her unresponsiveness only deepened his sense of helplessness. The task of carrying both Emily and the mysterious sword proved too formidable for him to do alone. In a twist of fate, just when Ethan wished for assistance, Lily emerged at the scene, providing an unexpected glimmer of hope.

Lily and Ethan carefully transported Emily to Ethan's home, where his parents stood ready to attend to her. Once inside, Emily was gently placed on a bed, and in the fleeting moments of consciousness, she managed to sip some water offered by Ethan's parents.

Curiosity tugging at her, Lily inquired, "Why didn't the controller send a car or a truck to pick up Emily? It would have been much easier than us bringing her here on bicycles."

Ethan pondered for a moment before responding, "I was wondering the same thing. But then I realized that I hadn't seen any vehicles being driven by anyone in this Call of Dream period. It's as if the entire world has chosen a simpler mode of living during this time."

As the two friends contemplated the changes in the world during this peculiar period, Lily posed a question, "So… the controller does not know how to drive a car?"

Ethan considered her inquiry, responding with a thoughtful expression, "Hmm… Could be, but I think it has something to do with protecting the environment from pollution."

Lily nodded in agreement, acknowledging, "Ohh, yeah, that makes better sense."

Curious about Lily's return, Ethan asked, "Why didn't you go to the marvelous place?"

Lily explained, "Two streets. That's the most I could cross. After that, I was completely blocked by people and got redirected towards you. The unexpected act of redirection seemed important and urgent, so I followed the guidance."

Ethan rushed upstairs to retrieve the books that they had borrowed from the library, earlier that day. He meticulously searched for references about the peculiar sword in the book, finding numerous drawings, and depictions within the pages. The descriptions hinted at a metal unfamiliar to their world, adding an extra layer of intrigue. Although the books lacked an extensive history of the sword, various pieces of evidence pointed to its ancient origins.

As they delved deeper into their research, Emily regained consciousness.

Unfortunately, she had no recollection of the recent incident. However, as she began recounting the events that happened after her last meeting with Ethan, the revelations left both Ethan and Lily in a state of shock.

Anabelle recounted her experience, revealing that on her way back home, she halted at the marvelous place upon hearing an unusual noise. Engulfed in darkness, she proceeded cautiously, driven by curiosity, in the hope that it might be Marcus. However, the closer she got, the more she discerned that the source of the sound could not possibly be Marcus. Instead, it resembled the sound of an animal breathing heavily. The mysterious atmosphere heightened her anxiety as she ventured further into the unknown.

Suddenly, a resonant thud echoed through the air, and Anabelle's heart skipped a beat. A colossal red creature, unlike anything she had ever seen, shifted its massive leg nearby. In the shadow of the immense foot, she felt minuscule and vulnerable. Paralyzed with fear, her mind raced for a course of action, and in desperation, she whispered a prayer to the universe, seeking salvation from the impending danger.

Attempting to blend into the surroundings, Anabelle hoped to go unnoticed by the colossal creature. However, her efforts proved futile as the creature's gaze fell upon her, locking eyes with the bewildered and terrified Anabelle.

Anabelle's trip down memory lane was interrupted by the gentle touch of Ethan's father, whose hands rested on the shoulders of both Anabelle and Ethan. Their attention was redirected to the dining table, realizing that it was time for dinner.

Unbeknownst to Lily and Anabelle, Ethan had a hypothesis he wished to put to the test. Instructing Lily and Anabelle to hold off on eating, he initiated the experiment.

As the parents eagerly waited to commence their meal, Ethan took the first bite. However, instead of joining in, their parents' eyes shifted to Emily. Recognizing the pivotal moment, Ethan encouraged Emily to start eating. Miraculously, as soon as Emily began, his parents resumed their meal. Though Lily and Emily were perplexed by Ethan's actions, he had successfully substantiated his theory. Ethan believed that his parents were waiting for their children to start eating before they began, offering tangible proof that Anabelle was indeed Emily, even if she had no recollection of it.

After a satisfying dinner, Ethan's father gestured towards the main door, placing his hands on both Ethan's and Emily's shoulders. The unspoken message was clear – they had a destination to reach. Ethan, Anabelle, and Lily stepped outside, greeted by the sight of three bicycles. Assuming the third one was for Anabelle, they embarked on their journey in the direction pointed out by Ethan's mother.

Curious, Lily inquired, "So, how did you manage to escape from that massive creature?"

Anabelle casually responded, "He saw me and asked if I wanted some meat to eat."

The unexpected nature of Anabelle's encounter made Ethan momentarily lose his grip on the pedal, causing his leg to slip. Swiftly recovering, he sought clarification, "Are you joking?"

Anabelle recounted, "No, I am not. I was just as shocked as you are now when the creature spoke. It even offered to barbeque the meat for me if I preferred it. For a moment, I thought it considered me as the meat and was informing me of its intention to devour me. But then it pointed to another creature lying dead beside it. It claimed to have slain that beast in a battle and expressed its desire to taste the flesh of Dragoor, citing a 900-year-old rivalry.

The creature asked if I understood the human fascination with names ending in 'oor,' as all the creatures it encountered had names like that. I was mesmerized by a massive creature with sharp teeth, a long mouth, small hands, and big legs talking to me. It even explained that its ability to talk and its current form were the result of a curse from its father.

The creature shared, and I quote, 'My father is the Creator and the Guardian of Gardoon, he cursed me to assume this creature's form, a creation his subordinates had been working on to deploy on another planet. He cursed me to live on this planet until he sent his blood to free me from this form with the weapon he forged with his own hands. DIE NO SOR – That was the last word I heard from him. I still do not know what it meant.' The creature did not speak as if it belonged to this world. It spoke about souls traversing from a higher dimension to worlds like ours and how it used to be the purifier of sinful souls."

Hearing Anabelle's account triggered a realization in Ethan that the creature his sister had encountered might indeed be Kargoor. However, the descriptions did not match the stories he had heard. In Ethan's understanding, Kargoor was a formidable monster known for wreaking havoc and destruction. He found it hard to relate this image with the creature Emily described, leading him to doubt whether his sister had truly encountered Kargoor.

Lily, curious about the connection between Emily and the mysterious sword, asked, "How did you come into possession of that sword?"

Anabelle recounted, "My memory about that sword is a complete blank for me. I just remember some events before it. After that night, I fell asleep, and upon waking, I found myself near the wall surrounding our town."

Ethan brought his bicycle to a halt and inquired, "You could see the protective wall surrounding our town?"

Anabelle and Lily stopped their bicycles as well. Anabelle confirmed, "Uh… Yes? Can't you?"

Ethan glanced at Lily and then back at Anabelle, explaining, "We read that the magic wall is visible only to those possessing magical abilities."

Anabelle's face lit up with excitement. "Do you think I have magic?" she asked eagerly.

Ethan and Lily nodded in agreement.

Filled with joy, Anabelle closed her eyes and made a wish, "I wish for a bowl of ice cream with one scoop of chocolate, one scoop of butterscotch, and one scoop of blueberry, topped with nuts, and chocolate sauce, served in a crisp waffle cone with a dollop of whipped cream!"

Disappointment washed over her as nothing appeared in her hands. Lily remarked, "I guess that's not how your magic works."

Both turned to Ethan, who looked even more disappointed than Lily. "I was looking forward to that," he sighed. "Now I can't get the image of that ice cream out of my mind."

Lily interjected, "Our town's safety is at stake, and you both are thinking about ice cream? That too three scoops, no less?"

Ethan leaned toward Emily and whispered, "She talks as if she's never had ice cream before. But let's strike a deal, once you figure out how to use your magic, wish for two bowls."

Anabelle whispered back, "I'm not even sure if I have magic."

Before they could continue their conversation, Lily interrupted, "What are you two discussing?"

Both of them replied simultaneously, "Nothing," and resumed riding.

Lily interrogated, "Ethan! I still remember the conversation about the magic wall and the colossal creatures we had back in the library. Do you think I possess magic as well?"

Ethan replied, "I am not sure. But we'll know once we are at the wall."

Anabelle continued, "Hmmm… Where was I? Oh yeah, I remember. I saw the wall. The wall was broken, revealing a forest outside—eighty percent green and twenty percent brown. The red creature stood beside the hole, concealing itself, waiting for something to enter through the breach. In a hushed tone, he asked me to be quiet, explaining that he was anticipating his breakfast. His whisper, given his immense size, was still quite loud.

Suddenly, another creature, Sargoor, this one blue and half the size of the red one, entered through the wall. Kargoor's face lit up with joy at the sight of Sargoor. Despite the blue one's attempts to retreat, Kargoor blocked its path, and it darted into the town. Without hesitation, I sprinted in a random direction, covering a vast distance. At one point, Sargoor was about to trample me. I closed my eyes. That is the last thing I remember. When I opened my eyes again, I was in Ethan's house."

Ethan inquired, "The wall is broken? Where is that place?"

Anabelle responded, "It's near the marvelous place. We can go there now. Maybe we can find the red creature there."

The trio halted at the spot where Ethan had spotted the rose earlier that morning beneath the lone tree. Dismounting their bicycles, they proceeded on foot toward the location of Dragoor's skull, leaving the sword behind, completely forgotten about it. As they approached, a glow became visible, and Anabelle exclaimed that it was the marvelousness she had mentioned.

She sprinted towards the light with Ethan and Lily in tow. Drawing closer, they discovered that the light emanated from myriad small luminescent butterflies. The entire area was teeming with them, casting an enchanting glow over Dragoor's skeletal remains. Ethan comprehended why his sister had dubbed it a marvelous place.

Nobody felt inclined to depart from the magical scene. Hence, they opted against visiting the broken wall during the nocturnal hours when visibility would be compromised. Instead, they resolved to spend the night amid the enchantment of that marvelous place.

As they all gazed at the radiant fireflies, Ethan found himself in the center. To his left stood Lily, and to his right, Emily. A familiar sensation gripped him as he recalled the similar dreams he had. It dawned on him that the girl on his right, whose visage remained elusive, was none other than his sister.

The origin and nature of these butterflies remained a mystery to everyone present. Eager to examine Dragoor's skull bathed in the ethereal glow, Ethan, and Lily moved in for a closer look. However, the surreal ambiance triggered memories of Marcus for Anabelle, freezing her in place.

Lily, catching a glimpse of Emily, was utterly astounded by what she witnessed. Silently approaching Ethan, she tapped his shoulder and directed his attention towards his sister. Ethan, beholding his sister, felt a profound sense of awe, surpassing even the marvel they had witnessed moments ago.

Anabelle gazed sorrowfully at the ground, her thoughts consumed by Marcus. The tiny, radiant butterflies gathered behind Lily, creating a magnificent wing that seemed to rest upon an invisible angelic aura surrounding Emily. At that poignant moment, Ethan grasped the realization that every unfolding event was intricately connected to a grander purpose, with his sister at the epicenter!

That night, in the ethereal realm of dreams, Ethan found himself standing at the center of a bridge he traversed daily on his way to college. The waters beneath the bridge sparkled crystal clear, devoid of the plastic pollution that marred reality. A jubilant fish leaped joyfully, dipping back into the pristine river. An elusive call beckoned from his right, leading him to turn in vain. As he faced forward, Lily appeared on his left, her eyes gleaming with delight at the sight of the unpolluted river.

A sudden, powerful grip seized his left shoulder, wrenching him towards the source. To Ethan's astonishment, his psychology professor stood before him. In the dream, an otherworldly roar erupted from his professor's mouth, resembling a monstrous cry, jolting him awake and bringing an end to the dream.

As Ethan turned to gaze at the peaceful slumber of Lily and Emily nestled within Dragoor's skull, a newfound calm enveloped him. Stepping out into the day, he discovered the luminescent butterflies had vanished and were replaced by an eerie yet familiar creature's sound that echoed his recent dream. Urgently rousing Lily and Emily, they followed the haunting sound, their feet carrying them to the broken wall.

Before them, the wall unfolded like a revelation, captivating their eyes with its enigmatic presence. In a dramatic entrance, Kargoor emerged from behind the wall, exhaling a gentle wisp of fire. Ethan and Lily stood in awe, eyes widened, breath caught in their throats, as the colossal, crimson creature, capable of breathing fire, materialized before them.

Kargoor's eyes gleamed with delight upon spotting Anabelle, addressing her with a mix of affection and triumph, "My princess. Finally, you are here, and right on time. You made it very easy for me to get my delightful breakfast yesterday. Without you, I would not have tasted the blue beast, Sourtail. I have always wanted to taste him from the moment I sensed the evilness in him about 500 years ago. He was fast, so he always managed to escape from me. But not yesterday and the credit goes to my princess, Anabelle."

Kargoor saw the state of Emily and Lily and he said, "Princess, can you tell your friends to relax? It seems like their eyeballs are on the verge of popping out of their sockets."

Although Ethan and Lily couldn't relax completely, their eyes returned to normal.

Anabelle, however, needed answers. She questioned Kargoor, "Did I assist you in killing that blue creature?"

Kargoor, with a hint of pride, replied, "Indeed, you did. Do you doubt that Sourtail would have survived after what you did to that filthy creature yesterday?"

Anabelle looked at Ethan and Lily, then back at Kargoor, inquiring, "Can you provide more details on what I did?"

Kargoor, with a mocking tone, asked, "Ah, are you seeking specifics to impress your friends with your coolness?"

Anabelle clarified, "No, it's not that. I can't recall what happened during that time. That's why I'm asking you."

Kargoor shared, "I started chasing that wretched beast, preventing him from escaping back into the forest. His strength lies in his speed. I pursued him, and after some time, he charged right at you. I feared he would trample you, but your actions astounded me. I've existed in this world in this form for a millennium. Believe me, I've witnessed things I shouldn't have. Yet, what you did was unprecedented. You leaped directly at that creature just as he was about to stomp on you. From my vantage point behind him, I couldn't discern the details, but it appeared as if you struck his throat, and suddenly, the fire started pouring out, consuming the entire vicinity.

I never imagined that vile creature could unleash such power. I saw you ascend, unburned, holding something in your hand. So, I chased the creature out of the wall. However, he succumbed just a few steps beyond his newfound freedom. It dawned on me that your blow was lethal. I merely extracted his life force and devoured him whole. I advise you all to stay clear of the right side of this wall by approximately fifty feet—by fifty feet, I mean my feet, not yours. That's where I took care of business this morning. Even that smells akin to the filth in that creature. Even after his death, his filth stayed back."

After Kargoor finished recounting the events, Anabelle struggled to comprehend what he had disclosed.

The perplexity of hearing about her actions, coupled with the absence of any recollection, left her in a state of bewilderment.

Kargoor added, "Had you stayed back yesterday, you could have savored that Sourtail. Despite his filth, he tasted truly exceptional. Very good, believe me. Except for his tail, it had a sour taste, hence the name Sourtail. I've never experienced anything quite like it before. It was well worth the wait."

While narrating his tale, Kargoor noticed the intensity in Ethan's and Lily's gaze fixated on the gap in the wall. Their eyes widened as they witnessed a large white creature, Henasaur, charging towards them. As the creature approached the wall, Kargoor positioned himself in its path. Despite attempting to slow down, the white creature could not avert its course. With swift precision, Kargoor clamped down on the creature's throat, hoisting it into the air with the strong muscles in his neck and his back.

In a forceful display, he slammed the creature to the ground, employing his leg to deliver a fatal stomp to its chest. The creature's demise was sealed as Kargoor swiftly bit into its neck, separating its head from its body.

After the kill, Kargoor did not reflect satisfaction. He said, "The worst breakfast came searching for me. I myself have killed and eaten almost a million of this

Henasaur's family. And I still have no idea where they come from."

Turning towards the three witnesses who were yet to return to their usual state after witnessing the brutal killing, Kargoor commented, "Unlucky day for us all."

He then opened his mouth and exhaled fire that engulfed the creature, barbequing every part of the creature.

He declared, "Leave the head. Except for that, you all can have anything. Guests first. Dig in. I wanted to say enjoy. But I couldn't. So, all of you say your thanks to my father for sending me here, making you all present here when I killed this creature, and be happy that you are getting good nutrition in this flesh."

Chapter 6

Angel or Demon

The three hesitated at first, unsure about consuming the charred remains of the creature. However, curiosity overcame their apprehension, and they cautiously began to eat. To their surprise, the creature's flesh tasted remarkably like chicken and nothing worse, contrary to Kargoor's earlier remark.

Anabelle broke the silence, expressing her satisfaction, "It tastes like chicken. What's not to like? I'm enjoying it." Ethan and Lily nodded in agreement with Emily's assessment.

Kargoor was astonished that the three found the white creature's meat palatable. Unfamiliar with the concept of chicken, he realized that humans had not experienced tasty meat in a long time.

Lily added, "Actually, this meat is even better than chicken!"

Kargoor understood that what seemed like an unpleasant breakfast for him was a satisfying meal for the other three. He began devouring the creature, starting with its head. By the time the three had finished their breakfast, Kargoor had meticulously consumed every bit of flesh, leaving almost only the bones behind.

Once the unusual feast concluded, Ethan could not resist his curiosity as to how a fierce heartless monster turned into the one they were looking at. But he had to put the town's state in front of his thoughts, so he asked Kargoor, "Do you know why there is a wall around this town, and how it was built?"

Kargoor, reminiscing, responded, "Oh yes, how can I forget that day! It was the day my bad time started. The wall was built on the day I was punished and sent to this world."

"We call ourselves Devarnams. We, led by my father, are responsible for looking after Gardoon. I was entrusted with the responsibility of delivering punishments to the souls that had sinned during their time on this planet. My role garnered hatred from many, yet I understood the gravity of my duty. My father, recognizing my efficiency, had entrusted me with this responsibility. However, I made a grave mistake—I betrayed the trust placed in me and assisted Vaulmour in evading the punishment for the sins she had committed. Vaulmour was more than just a friend. She broke the love I had for her when she tricked me and my mother and helped unleash darkness onto our universe, Kan. All because she wanted to rule Gadroon.

When darkness loomed over all the worlds like ours, a collective effort was made to combat the threat. I actively participated in the war against the demons that spread the darkness. Although the war concluded, the aftermath saw me vilified and despised by all, for I played a significant role in unleashing evil 1200 years ago. As a punitive measure and to instill in me the value of my duty, my father cursed me to be born in this world.

At the time when this town's protective wall was raised, powerful individuals from other realms were summoned here to construct it with magic. Initially, I believed the wall's purpose was to shield the people from me, but only recently did I come to understand its true intent from a traveler named Narad, who travels across universes. He said that the walls were not built to protect the people from me; instead, they were erected to safeguard an ancient artifact from the resurgence of that darkness. This revelation implies that the darkness has regained strength, posing a threat to this world."

Upon hearing this, Ethan's uncertainty about his ability to confront the encroaching darkness intensified, casting a shadow over his confidence.

Lily, concerned about the impending threat, exclaimed, "So, you're saying this darkness could wipe out everyone in the town? Why are we just sitting here then? Shouldn't we be figuring out a way to rebuild the wall? Why does the wall only cover the sides and not the top?"

Kargoor, with a reassuring tone, said, "Don't worry, trying to rebuild the wall would be impossible. Unless one of you possesses the secrets to the ancient magics of Gardoon. Which is far beyond the capabilities of even my father. And honestly, I am not sure why the wall does not cover the top. Maybe the danger doesn't come from above. In all my time in Gardoon in this form, I've only seen one flying creature: a golden dragon. I don't know where it came from or where it went, I saw it only once. But there's no need to panic too much. My father is good at dealing with situations like these. Nothing happens randomly. I, being in this creature's form, serve a purpose. If my instincts are right, he must have already started a plan to save lives on this planet. Have any of you noticed or felt anything strange happening lately?"

A puzzled silence enveloped them as the three companions contemplated Kargoor's question and kept looking at him.

Kargoor said, "Apart from encountering me."

Ethan shared, "Yeah, it's been strange. Everyone's acting oddly, raising their hands. Even the animals have been relocated. And, strangely, we are the only normal ones remaining."

Kargoor pondered, "Humans with raised hands, you say? This reminds me of the time when the wall was being constructed. I wonder if my brother, Zendayan has a hand in this."

Anabelle voiced her concern, "What about Marcus? He was like us, but he suddenly vanished, claiming he was being controlled and heard voices in his head."

Kargoor expressed his worry, "Voices in the head. Oh no, that person might be in danger. I cannot say for certain, but there's a possibility that he's under the influence of a demon from the darkness."

Upon hearing this, Anabelle became somber, and tears welled up in her eyes. Kargoor noticed the sadness on Anabelle's face and offered consolation saying, "Everything is happening for a reason. Perhaps, me being here and you all meeting with me is part of the plan."

Lily, grappling with the idea, questioned, "I don't understand. If everything is unfolding as it should, does it mean that we're all being controlled by someone to carry out a predetermined script? Are we just actors following a script?"

Kargoor grinned, but due to his monstrous form, the smile took a terrifying turn. Seeing the terror in their eyes, Kargoor, aware of the effect, remarked, "Oh my. I never knew my smile was this terrifying!"

Kargoor continued his explanation, "Yes, dear. Consider your life in this world as a script—a narrative designed to bring you to precise moments where you need to be. Events unfold as they should, but your actions in those moments are entirely your own. The scripts are crafted to give you a chance to fulfill your purpose in life and to learn the lessons from your time here. Ultimately, it's our free will that determines our choices and actions."

Ethan, seeking deeper understanding, inquired, "But why is all of this happening? Where did we come from? Why are we in these forms and what is our purpose in life?"

Kargoor fixed his eyes on Ethan, his silence carrying the weight of unspoken thoughts. After a moment, he spoke, "I wish I knew. Unfortunately, I'm not in a position to answer your questions. When I took this creature's form, my memories faded. I can only recall fragments of my past—specifically, the last chapter of my story before arriving on this planet. Memories of helping Vaulmour and facing my father's punishment are the clearest, but the rest is a blur."

Lily pondered and asked, "If our purpose is to fulfill our life's mission, why don't we remember it? Having a clear understanding of our purpose would enable us to navigate life more effectively, right? So, why are our memories of life before this existence erased?"

Kargoor responded, "Hmm, an intriguing question. I've thought about it myself. Unfortunately, lacking those memories, I cannot provide you with an exact answer. However, during my time on this planet, I learned something. I witnessed the beauty of this planet, thanks to my mother and sister for creating such a remarkable place. I never comprehended it before and never appreciated her. Perhaps, that could be one reason. If we descended here with knowledge of what we should be doing, it would be a form of control as we would be influenced by predetermined tasks. During our time here, we might overlook the beauty of this world, nature, and all that unfolds, as our focus would be directed elsewhere. This could be a reason why we do not arrive with memories. I now appreciate my mother and sister's creation."

Ethan observed his sister, deep in thought, and seemingly preoccupied with something concerning Marcus. Concerned, he turned to Kargoor and inquired, "You mentioned darkness. What are its capabilities, and what might its plans be with Marcus? How can we prepare ourselves to fight against it?"

Recognizing Anabelle's distress, Kargoor directed his question toward her, "Could you provide more details about the activities and incidents Marcus was involved in?"

All eyes focused on Emily, and she shared, "He had been hearing voices for a while, managing to overcome them most of the time. However, it escalated at the marvelous place for the first time. He claimed that someone was attempting to control him."

Kargoor contemplated the revelations, saying, "From what you've described, it seems like you are the chosen protectors of this world. Typically, only one, or two individuals are sent to safeguard the world during times like these. But why are there four of you? That's something I can't fathom. Marcus's behavior appears to be unprecedented, something I haven't encountered or, perhaps, don't remember. Now, what's the significance of the marvelous place? Why is it so extraordinary?"

Lily, filled with excitement, eagerly began recounting her experiences at the marvelous place. Kargoor, however, seemed perplexed and inquired, "It occurs only at night, is it? But I was there when I killed Dragoor in that place at night. Why couldn't I see the luminous butterflies? This could only mean one thing. To confirm, we have to be at the marvelous place tonight. Tonight might be the night it happens. The last time I witnessed it, it was followed by an unpleasant event. The only thing I'm uncertain about is Marcus. I can't seem to relate him to anyone."

Anabelle, with a compassionate gaze, asked, "What happened the last time you saw the luminous butterflies?"

Kargoor took a deep breath, the weight of his memories evident in his eyes. He spoke somberly, "I lost my love and my son. And I wished not to encounter that luminous butterfly again."

Continuing his tale, Kargoor recounted, "About 750 years ago, I was nothing but a remorseless killing machine, driven solely by hunger and devoid of purpose. If I hadn't met her, I would have remained that relentless monster. She changed everything. She gave me a reason to live, accepted the monster within me, and envisioned a better path for us. Despite knowing her time was limited, she wished to spend her life with me, believing she could lift the curse. But I lost her, along with our son. I still blame myself for what had happened that day. That was the day I saw the luminous butterflies for the last time. They sat on their dead bodies and glowed brightly. I did not have the nerve to look at them. I began searching for a way to end my life in this world. But I couldn't. I just feel like I do not deserve them."

As Kargoor poured out his heart, tears streamed down his eyes, falling helplessly to the ground. His short hands struggled to wipe away the emotions, and the inability to control his tears only intensified the moment. Suddenly, the sky responded with a downpour, as if nature itself empathized with Kargoor's sorrow. Raindrops mingled with his tears, making his tears invisible to the others. Looking skyward, Kargoor uttered, "It hurts you to see your son in tears, isn't it? Then why did you not give me the chance to see my son grow? I never understood your plans and games. It is just so hurtful."

Lily looked up at the pouring sky and wondered to herself, "Maybe it's the rain. The wall does not cover the top so that the towns receive rain."

The rain showed no signs of abating, prompting the three to seek refuge beneath Kargoor. This impromptu shelter provided them relief from the relentless downpour. An hour later, as the rain ceased, Kargoor's stomach growled audibly. Lily, bemused, questioned, "Just an hour ago, you ate a large creature for breakfast. And now you're hungry again?"

Kargoor grinned and replied, "Everyone used to say that my stomach and heart are too big."

Ethan, attempting to lighten the mood, quipped, "Just a request. Can you please let us know the next time you smile? I would rather know that you are smiling than look at it. It is terrifying."

Kargoor halted his grin and retorted, "Why create a creature that could not smile? After I return, I am going to destroy all these creatures that look similar to me, from all the planets and create new ones that can smile."

Anabelle, intrigued by the conversation, interjected, "Can you create humans with wings?"

Kargoor calmly responded, "They are already there. It's a pretty old design. It did not end up good for humans. I want to create a creature that has a smile that makes anyone smile out of happiness just by looking at it."

Anabelle reminisced, "Marcus has… had… such a smile."

Sensing the somberness, Ethan decided to lighten the mood. He proposed taking a walk outside the wall to explore the world beyond. Kargoor seemed to agree with him as he said, "in search of lunch."

At first, Emily hesitated, unsure of what to expect. But Lily's enthusiasm proved to be infectious. With her persuasive charm, Lily convinced her to embark on this unexpected adventure, with the understanding that they would return immediately if anything seemed amiss.

Upon stepping outside the wall, the trio could instantly sense the difference in the air—fresh and invigorating. Lily could not contain her excitement and exclaimed, "I can't believe I have missed this my whole life."

Under Kargoor's careful supervision, they ventured into the unknown, ready to explore the wonders that existed beyond the familiar confines of their town.

Kargoor, offering a word of caution, said, "Don't be fooled by the pleasantness. Sometimes the most pleasant thing in nature could be the most dangerous thing for us."

He led them to a nearby waterfall, chosen not only for its natural beauty but also as a potential source of food. Kargoor explained that creatures often frequented the area for water. The soothing sound of the waterfall put the trio in a meditative state, but their tranquillity was disrupted by an unsettling noise—an approaching creature.

The sound grew louder, prompting Kargoor to caution, "Here comes our lunch. You all get down and hide behind a tree. I hope it's not the white creature family again."

Kargoor braced himself, sensing the urgency in the creature's distressed call. The unusual timbre of its cry signaled danger, hinting that something more formidable might be pursuing it. As he pondered the potential threats lurking nearby, a familiar sight caught his eye: a white creature running aggressively in his direction.

A sigh escaped Kargoor's lips, a mix of frustration and resignation. "Not again," he muttered under his breath, preparing for yet another encounter with a white creature.

As Kargoor observed the scene unfolding before him, the white creature attempted to change its course upon spotting him. However, it was intercepted by another creature that swiftly seized its neck from behind, causing it to stumble. With a calculated move, the pursuing creature took advantage of the white creature's imbalance, clamping down on its neck until life extinguished.

Kargoor stood frozen, witnessing the ruthless efficiency of a pickle-green colored creature that mirrored his form. The trio, concealed behind the tree, mirrored his astonishment as their eyes oscillated between Kargoor and the doppelganger. The doppelganger, before getting on with its lunch, felt the presence of another creature in the perimeter. It turned its attention to Kargoor, unleashing a guttural shout before swiftly darting away. The unexpected encounter left Kargoor in a state of disbelief, pondering the implications of the creature's striking resemblance to himself. Grappling with the shock of encountering a creature resembling himself, he tried to come to terms with the possibilities surrounding its existence.

Upon calling out to Kargoor, it took a few moments for him to reorient himself. Ethan proposed pursuing the mysterious creature, while Lily, alarmed by its trajectory toward their town, urged immediate action.

Kargoor, understanding the urgency, bent down for the trio to climb onto his hand. With a firm grip, he instructed them to hold tight as he embarked on the chase. The enigmatic creature, slightly outpacing Kargoor, seemed to possess an elusive speed. Kargoor, mindful of the towering trees and potential danger, refrained from reaching his maximum speed, wary of the consequences a fall from such heights could pose to the humans in his care.

Kargoor could not catch up with the creature bearing a striking resemblance to him. The creature swiftly entered the town through the breach in the wall, sending waves of terror through Kargoor and the three witnesses. As Kargoor entered the town, frantic in his pursuit, the mysterious creature seemed to vanish without a trace.

Returning to the hole in the wall, Kargoor attempted to follow the creature's path. The footprints were distinguishable, revealing a smaller size than his own. The tracks abruptly disappeared a few meters from the wall, leaving Kargoor perplexed.

Expressing his confusion, Kargoor said, “I was under the impression that my character’s design was unique, a test by my father. I can’t fathom how a creature of that size could simply vanish from our sight.”

Inquisitively, Lily suggested, “Could it have appeared and disappeared with magic?”

Kargoor pondered, “Hmm. Maybe. Maybe the creature is not from this world. Perhaps it’s connected to the darkness. However, I wouldn’t worry too much about it. I’m confident that safety measures are already in place. What concerns me now is my lunch. I may not act like myself when I’m hungry.”

Lily suggested, “What if you go back and eat that white creature?”

Kargoor responded, “I’ve never consumed the kill of another creature. But given the current situation, I don’t want to miss out on my father’s plans. So, I’ll see you all in a bit once my stomach is satisfied. You keep an eye out for that creature.”

With that, Kargoor departed. Ethan, Emily, and Lily, realizing they had left the sword near the bicycle the previous day, hurriedly ran toward the location, hoping to retrieve it before Kargoor’s return. However, to their disappointment, they were met with a surprise – the sword was missing.

Anabelle questioned, “Who could have taken the sword?”

Ethan admitted, "No idea. We made a grave mistake by leaving it here last night."

Lily quickly intervened, saying, "OK. Now is not the time to worry about the mistakes of the past. Let's think about what we can do next. Who do you both think could have taken the sword?"

Understanding the futility of dwelling on past mistakes, Ethan remarked, "There's a lesser possibility that anyone who is under the influence of the Call of Dream could have taken it."

Anabelle sought clarification, "Call of Dream?"

Lily explained, "The phenomenon where people are walking with their hands raised is called the Call of Dream."

Ethan continued, "Why I consider it a lesser possibility is that if someone had taken it, they should have given it to us when we arrived here. The only reason for someone under the Call of Dream to take the sword is if the controller didn't want us to have it for some reason."

Lily pondered, "What if the magician creature took it?"

Ethan speculated, "If the creature is a magician and was aware of the abilities of the sword, it might have taken it."

Anabelle sought clarification, "Wait. What about the sword? What is so special about it?"

Ethan explained, "There are several magical swords mentioned in ancient books. Some can pierce through anything, others can control water, air, rock, and fire, while one can attract negative energy. Our sword seems to be one of those magical blades, specifically one that creates and controls fire."

Ethan turned towards Emily and asked, "Can you try a little to recollect something more about the sword."

Anabelle struggled to recollect the incident, but her memory proved elusive. The more she strained to remember, the more fatigued she became. Ethan persistently urged her to recall the moment, ignoring Lily's attempts to convey Emily's struggle. As the insistence continued, Anabelle grew tired, eventually collapsing to the ground.

Chapter 7

What an Incredible Gift

Anabelle, in her unconscious state, experienced a vivid dream or vision. Though the details were unclear, upon awakening, she found herself inside Dragoor's skull. Ethan and Lily had carried her there for shade and rest after she fainted due to Ethan's persistent inquiries. Stepping out of the skull, she discovered Ethan and Lily engaged in a heated argument about Ethan's actions that led to her fainting.

Anabelle questioned, "How long was I unconscious?"

Lily replied, "About an hour."

Anabelle exclaimed, "An hour! Wow. Where is Kargoor? Has he not returned yet?"

Lily responded, "No."

Ethan sincerely apologized for pressuring Emily to remember the incident, but she assured him it wasn't his fault. She expressed a genuine desire to understand the pivotal moment that might unveil crucial aspects of her identity, refraining from placing blame on Ethan.

Anabelle proceeded to share the details of her vision. She described finding herself in a void or what could have been a night when a brilliant light appeared and spoke to her. However, she couldn't recognize the voice. She also revealed having a similar dream before the onset of the Call of Dream, where she gazed at something bright that made it challenging to see. In that instance, she had to shield her eyes from the arm of someone nearby to protect them from the overwhelming brightness.

Upon hearing Anabelle's account of her visions, both Ethan and Lily stared at her in astonishment. Simultaneously, they exclaimed, "You had that dream too?"

Anabelle, bewildered, asked, "What do you mean? Did you both have the same dream as well?"

Lily confirmed, saying, "Yes, I experienced that blinding light at night, and it bothered my eyes. I witnessed it just the day before the Call of Dream began. However, I don't recall seeing you there, it was just Ethan."

Ethan playfully inquired, "So, does that mean you were thinking about me that night before you slept?"

Lily responded, "What? No… You're just my college mate. Just because you volunteered first doesn't mean I'd be thinking about you."

Ethan retorted, "Ahh, no. Similarly, I wasn't thinking about you that night either."

A brief, awkward silence lingered between Ethan and Lily until Anabelle interjected, saying, "And I was not thinking about either of you. I guess you both have made your point. Let's come back to the present now?"

Ethan explained, "Yeah, right. In my dream, I saw both of you. Lily was on my left, and on my right was a girl whose face I couldn't see. If we piece together our dreams, it seems like the three of us witnessed the same light."

Lily, perplexed, questioned, "How is that even possible? What could that light be? Is it Kargoor's father? God himself?"

Anabelle pondered, "Maybe we'll have to wait for Kargoor to describe what his father looks like."

Ethan added, "I have a feeling that we're at the center of something huge, but we're just not sure what it is."

While they were engrossed in conversation, Kargoor arrived in search of them. Anabelle quizzed him, "What took you so long?"

Kargoor sighed, "Your towns are doomed. I went back to eat that Henosaur. After finishing it, I was about to return when I heard a cry for help. It was the cry of a creature nearby, so I decided to check it out. When I arrived, I found five Henosaurs attacking another brown creature. They spotted me, and we engaged in a fierce battle. I managed to defeat all five of them. The creature that was under attack informed me that more Henosaurs were infiltrating the forest, killing everything in their path without consuming them—just killing and moving on."

Skeptically, Lily questioned, "You're kidding, right? Are you making up this story to cover up the fact that you leisurely enjoyed your lunch and took a nap?"

Anabelle chimed in, "Yeah, look at you. You claim to have fought five Henosaurs, but where are the signs of the fight on you?"

Kargoor turned around to reveal a canvas of bite marks on his back, evidence of the intense battle. He explained, "If the Henosaurs discover the hole in the wall, this town will be destroyed within minutes."

Concerned, Ethan asked, "What should we do now?"

Kargoor quickly responded, "I'll go around the town to check for any other holes in the wall. Then, I'll stand guard at this breach. Meanwhile, you all need to get everyone to safety, just in case the Henosaurs discover this opening."

Anabelle, puzzled, inquired, "You're Kargoor. You don't have any connection with our town. You don't need to protect this town. Why do you want to do it?"

Kargoor said, "I would have smiled and began to speak, but as you all are not welcoming my smile. You can imagine that I am smiling now as I speak. I've wandered this world for a millennium, living a seemingly purposeless existence—hunting, eating, walking, and sleeping. Everything changed when I met her. An angel, sent by my father, brought meaning to my life. The joy I experienced was linked to a newfound purpose – protecting my family. Sadly, I missed the chance to fulfill that duty. Now, it seems I've been granted a second opportunity. I'd rather face battles and endure wounds than witness a massacre."

Ethan added, "You should've smiled for that. We wouldn't have mocked you then."

Kargoor swiftly circled the town, inspecting the wall for any potential weak points. Meanwhile, the three of them made their way to their bicycles, intending to evacuate everyone to a safer location. Anabelle, amid the urgency, found herself feeling hungry. Upon reaching their bicycles, they were greeted by a person who handed them a sandwich-style lunch.

Taking a brief respite to eat, the mysterious person guided them to a vast hall designed to shelter the town's inhabitants during natural disasters. The hall was equipped with essentials to sustain people for several days. While it wasn't foolproof against the threat of the Henosaurs, there were some protective measures in place. Realizing that the townspeople were already gathered in the hall, the trio decided to return to the hole in the wall.

Upon their return, Kargoor had completed his inspection, confirming that there were no additional breaches in the wall apart from the one they knew of. Concerned for their safety, Kargoor advised the three to stay near Dragoor's skull while he stood guard at the hole in the wall.

The trio settled themselves close to Dragoor's skull, anxiously awaiting any signs of the looming threat. As the evening unfolded, there were no indications of the presence of Henosaurs. With the Sun setting and darkness enveloping the surroundings, Ethan contemplated the missing sword, speculating that it might have been taken for a more purposeful use. Reluctant to light a fire, fearing it would attract unwanted attention, they opted to stay inside Dragoor's skull to combat the chilly night.

As the night progressed and the clock approached midnight, an unexpected phenomenon unfolded. It began with the appearance of some small butterflies, followed by the emergence of larger, more radiant ones. Intrigued, the trio approached a tree from which the butterflies seemed to emanate. To their amazement, the tree appeared to be breathing, expanding, and shrinking rhythmically. Gradually, the expansion reached its zenith, revealing a majestic luminous butterfly emerging from what had initially seemed like a tree but was, in fact, a colossal cocoon.

The butterfly spread its wings wide, gracefully flapping them without venturing far from its original spot. Rather than flying away, it took a moment to introduce itself. In a melodic female tone, it spoke, "Greetings, people. I have many names, but among them, I am most commonly known as Margoor, the creator of life in this world. I had designed a fragment of me to take birth, live among you, and, when the time comes, assume this magnificent form to aid the ones that meet me in this form. While in this form, I possess the ability to provide answers to a single query of your choosing. You may inquire about anything—be it the past, the present, or the future. Once you pose your question, and I answer it, I will revert to my initial state until this transformation recurs after fifty years."

The three were captivated by the enchanting presence of Margoor and found themselves momentarily speechless. Recognizing their hesitancy, Margoor gently urged, "Come on, my friends. I cannot maintain this form forever."

Realizing the significance of their opportunity, the trio engaged in a brief discussion to ensure they made the most of their singular question. Eventually, Ethan spoke up, "We need to inquire about the sword."

Anabelle added, "And we must seek information about Marcus."

Lily chimed in, "We have to ask about the white creatures and the way to defeat them."

Anabelle contemplated, "What if we ask about the way to defeat the darkness itself?"

Lily asked, "Should we ask her why the invisible wall does not cover the top of our towns?"

Anabelle responded, "No, I feel like we should ask about Marcus."

As Lily and Anabelle delved into an intense discussion, Ethan maintained a thoughtful silence, thinking about a poignant story his mother once shared about the heartfelt wish of a poor, infertile blind man. In that story, the blind man, given the chance to make a wish, yearned to witness his children playing from the vantage point of the sixth floor of his house. A single wish to make sure all his problems are sorted. Ethan aimed to formulate a question akin to that blind man's wish.

However, before he could articulate his question, Margoor burst into laughter. The luminous butterfly playfully declared, "Apologies. I was just pulling your legs. I do not possess omniscient knowledge of the future while I am in this three-dimensional physical form. Even if I did, I would not be conveying it to you. Because if I did, you would lose interest in how the events would unfold. My purpose is to offer you a gift and convey a specific message."

The three exchanged puzzled glances, taking a few moments to grasp the nature of the message conveyed by the magnificent, luminous butterfly.

Margoor spoke, "The message is simple yet profound: Believe. Believe in yourselves. The universe loves you and will grant you the energy you seek. Your focus determines the energy you receive. Each of you was chosen for a reason. The power to save this world from darkness resides within all of you."

Lily, seeking more clarity, inquired, "Is that all? We just need to believe in ourselves?"

Margoor responded, "You may perceive it as simple, but achieving genuine self-belief can be a significant challenge. Keep this in mind. Tests will come your way; that's how the universe operates. It assesses you before granting your desires. In time, you'll understand why you were chosen. And Lily, to answer the question in your mind, yes, the wall does not cover the top as the living beings inside have to experience the beauty of rain, sun, moon and the night stars."

Lily asked, "So the golden dragon is not a threat?"

Margoor responded, "I wouldn't say so. It is a totally different story, you don't have to worry about it for now. All you have to do is take care of a creature called Vangoork."

Confusion clouded the expressions of the three friends as they exchanged glances.

Margoor continued, "Oh, I almost forgot. When I return to my initial form, I emit a dazzling light, drawing the attention of the darkness and initiating the battle between light and dark."

Ethan, feeling unprepared, nervously asked, "Is it not possible to reduce the intensity of the light emission? I don't think I'm ready for that."

Margoor reiterated, "Believing in yourself is key. You already possess what you need. All the problems you face are given to you only to the extent that you can handle. Consider it like this: you may not practice swimming every day, but when you find yourself in water, your body and mind recall the skill that helped you overcome the obstacle. It is the same with your soul. It will guide you through."

Expressing her fear, Lily questioned, "Our bodies are frail, and we are so small. What can we possibly do against those giant creatures?"

Margoor, sporting a reassuring smile, responded, "An elephant is afraid of ants. Have you ever wondered why? I'm confident you'll find the answer."

Ethan, still seeking assistance, inquired, "Can't you aid us in this fight against darkness?"

Margoor explained, "I genuinely wished to assist you in protecting my creation. However, you won't need my help. My father has orchestrated a plan for you. He strategically placed Kargoor on this side of the wall instead of the other. I owe gratitude to my father for sending that angel and altering my brother's life's path in this world."

Anabelle asked, "If this world is your creation. Doesn't it hurt you to see those Henosaurs being hurt by us?"

Margoor silently took in a deep breath and said in a faint voice, "It's like you read my mind. It hurts me a lot. But my creations are being manipulated by the darkness and are on the verge of destroying this world. But leave what happens to the souls that are to die in this fight. I will give them a better place for them to fulfill their life's purpose."

Before Ethan could ask another question, Margoor said, "Forgive me for stopping you, but I have less time left in this physical realm. I'll say what I have to say. All the help you need has been provided for you; all you have to do is believe and put your brain to better use. That is something we cannot enforce within you. Listen to your heart and soul. Believe in yourself, give everything you have, and never give up. With that said, it is time for me to take leave. Hoping to see you all in my next cycle!"

Margoor's luminous level became higher and higher. As she bloomed brightly, the three realized that Margoor was the source of light that they had seen in their dream. At the final moment, before Margoor disappeared, she said, "Oh, I almost forgot. I have left behind a present for you. And inform my brother that his son is alive."

The place became dark as Margoor's light disappeared. Well, she did not disappear, she began her next cycle. But the disappearance of her bright luminous light made the three blind for a moment and they could not see anything clearly for a couple of minutes. Everywhere they turned, they saw black patches as they looked into intense light.

Anabelle exaggerated, "Kargoor's son is alive!?"

Ethan pondered, "Could that creature we chased this afternoon that resembled Kargoor be his son?"

Lily stated, "Guess we might have an answer to why that creature was a mirror image of Kargoor."

Anabelle questioned, "So Kargoor's son can vanish into thin air?"

Struggling to see each other, their eye's photoreceptor cells, fatigued from exposure to the intense light, were readjusting.

Kargoor, sensing the brightness, hurried towards them and inquired, "What happened? What was that light?"

Anabelle replied, "It was your sister, Margoor."

Kargoor expressed confusion, "What? I don't have a sister named Margoor."

Lily clarified, "Your sister, the one who creates all life in this world. That's her."

Kargoor was taken aback, "What? My mother is the creator of life in Gardoon. She's the architect of nature itself. Oh, maybe my sister, Ira, should have taken over her position. Ira must be Margoor. Was she that bright light? What was she doing here?"

Ethan explained, "She came to deliver a message that can help us win the war."

Kargoor chuckled, "Let me guess. Did she ask you all to believe in yourselves?"

The three nodded affirmatively. Kargoor grinned, "Ah, I knew it. She tells the same to everyone. Even to me before I came here. But I already knew that. Our life on Gardoon is designed in a way to put us in difficult situations to teach us some lessons. What else did she say?"

Anabelle added, "She mentioned about your son."

Kargoor froze. All the 75 trillion cells in his body were in shock. His voice trembled as he questioned, "My son?"

Anabelle continued, "Your son is alive."

Kargoor's voice trembled, "No… No… Could it truly be? That is not possible. I saw my son fall in fire… But my sister does not lie. Could that mean that the creature that we were chasing today was my son?"

Lily nodded sympathetically, "That's the conclusion we're arriving at."

Kargoor's eyes filled with tears as he said, "My son is alive. Did she tell you where I can find him?"

Lily hesitated, "She didn't specify. She only mentioned that destiny would unveil everything when the moment is right."

Kargoor took a deep breath, his emotions swirling, "Oh wow, all these years I have been blaming my father for not letting my son live. But it seems he has written a different story for him. After all, it is his grandson. I hope he has crafted a brighter narrative for him."

Witnessing Kargoor's vulnerable moment, the trio felt a deep sense of empathy.

He quickly recomposed himself, stating, "Alright, emotions apart. I am taking my position at the hole, on watch. The bright light would have been easily noticed by the darkness. The Henosaurs might converge on us at any moment."

Pausing to glance at their surroundings, he queried, "By the way, what's that object before you? Did my sister leave it behind?"

Ethan promptly crouched down to search for the mysterious object Kargoor mentioned, given that his vision was yet to fully recover. Meanwhile, Lily and Anabelle, their eyes still adjusting, unintentionally swung their hands forward in an attempt to locate the object, inadvertently hitting Ethan's nose and shoulder in the process. Wincing from the impact, Ethan jokingly lamented, "What did I do to deserve this treatment?"

Apologies quickly followed from Lily and Anabelle, who expressed regret for the unintended collision. Sensing their struggle to see amid the lingering effects of the bright light and encroaching darkness, Kargoor took action. He uprooted a nearby tree and positioned it a distance away from the three of them, with the object being in the middle, before breathing fire onto it.

As the flames illuminated the surroundings, a magnificent sight unfolded before them—the revelation of a sword, firmly embedded in the ground, standing with a majestic presence. The fiery backdrop lent an enchanting glow to the discovery, leaving the trio in awe of the unexpected find.

Ethan could not contain his excitement, exclaiming, "What an incredible gift! We've reclaimed the lost sword."

Rushing towards the sword, he eagerly attempted to pull it from the ground. Despite his best efforts, the sword remained firmly embedded. Realizing the need for assistance, he turned to Kargoor, seeking his strength.

With a determined effort, Kargoor tried to move the sword with his massive legs, but he could not move it. He then placed his foot firmly on the ground and using his teeth attempted to pull it free. However, the sword stood its ground, leaving behind two distinct foot-shaped imprints in the earth.

Kargoor, perplexed and slightly frustrated, mused aloud. Then it hit his mind, shocked, he said, "This must be it. This is the weapon forged by my father himself, with his own hands. A weapon that could kill me. My father has finally sent his blood with the weapon to kill me. But why didn't she use it to end me?"

Lily, intrigued by the mystery, approached the sword for a closer examination. Circumventing it, she scrutinized every angle, searching for any invisible force holding it in place. Turning to Kargoor, she posed a speculative question, "Could there be an unseen organism, perhaps invisible, holding onto the sword?"

Kargoor dismissed the idea, stating, "There are a few of them, but even if there were a creature holding onto the sword, I could have easily lifted it."

Lily pondered for a moment before proposing an alternative, "What if we dig around the sword and unearth it from beneath?"

Ethan and Anabelle enthusiastically began digging around the sword while Kargoor maintained a cautious distance, still wary of the weapon. As they progressed, the solid rock beneath impeded their efforts. Undeterred, they split up to search for tools that could aid them. Lily, already fatigued, opted to take a moment to rest.

After a brief search, Ethan excitedly located a wooden stick that could facilitate their digging. Racing towards the sword, he called out to Lily. However, Lily, feeling a sudden numbness in her legs, attempted to rise using the sword for support. Unexpectedly, the sword came free from the ground, causing her to lose balance and fall backward. Ethan, unaware of what had transpired, continued running toward her, his initial shout replaced by a look of shock.

Upon reaching Lily, Ethan discovered her holding the sword. Sensing an unusual connection with the weapon, Lily found that it felt more like an extension of her hand than a mere object. Before she could fully comprehend the situation, Ethan requested the sword.

While relinquishing it to him, Lily witnessed an unexpected turn of events. The sword slipped from Ethan's grasp, proving too heavy for him to lift. Bewildered by the unfolding events, Ethan urged Lily to retrieve the sword. Remarkably, she effortlessly lifted the once-heavy weapon, leaving Ethan confused about the inexplicable shift in its weight.

Lily, with no prior experience in handling swords, found herself effortlessly maneuvering, and playing with the weapon. Surprising everyone, she skillfully plunged the sword into the ground, causing a rock to rise as if under her command. Witnessing this display of control, the onlookers realized that the sword possessed the ability to manipulate the surrounding rock elements. Lily, reveling in the joy of her newfound skills, radiated confidence.

On the contrary, Ethan felt a sense of unease, grappling with the inability to lift the once-burdened sword.

Lily asked if Kargoor had encountered a creature called Vangoork.

Kargoor responded, "Vangoork! No, never heard of that name."

Meanwhile, Kargoor, aware of the impending threat from the white creatures, needed to return to his post at the hole in the wall. Lily proposed joining him, suggesting they take turns standing guard to allow Kargoor some much-needed rest. Agreeing to the arrangement, Kargoor laid down one condition – that Lily keep the sword away from him.

As the duo walked towards the hole in the wall, Ethan and Anabelle stood in awe of Lily's transformation from a seemingly fragile girl to a bold, confident individual, ready to face the white creatures alone.

Ethan remarked, "I like what the sword did to her."

Anabelle concurred, "Yeah, it's like magic."

Chapter 8

Fire and Water

At the breach in the wall, Lily diligently practiced with her sword throughout the night without any rest. The night passed undisturbed, marked by an unusual calm. Lily attempted to conceal the hole in the wall by raising the rocks beneath, and while she could not entirely hide it, she managed to obscure it quite effectively, leaving a narrow path for Kargoor to move in and out of the wall.

As sunrise approached, Kargoor, awakening from his slumber, instructed Lily to return to the Dragoor's skull and take some rest.

The morning Sun brought Ethan back to consciousness, and as he observed his sister and Lily peacefully sleeping, the sword lying beside Lily triggered thoughts of his inability to lift it. Doubts crept into his mind, questioning whether he was chosen by mistake.

Stepping out of the skull, he proceeded with his morning routine. Upon returning, he found a wooden basket filled with fruits, bread, honey, and other provisions, distinct from the usual offerings. The selection felt purposeful, prompting Ethan to ponder its significance.

Anabelle, now awake and refreshed, joined Ethan for breakfast. After the meal, she expressed her intention to check on Kargoor. Ethan, opting to stay behind and protect Lily during her sleep, watched Anabelle leave.

Upon reaching Kargoor, Anabelle inquired, "Had a good sleep?"

Kargoor shared, "Yeah, had plenty of sleep. Lily did a good job guarding last night. I might not get much sleep today. I can sense those white creatures getting closer."

Anabelle inquired, "Did you eat anything? If the fight comes to us today, you need to have some energy. Did you have dinner last night?"

Kargoor responded, "Skipped dinner but had breakfast. People brought me some meat in carts as soon as I woke up. It was small but plentiful. It had two legs and tasted somewhat chemical. It was not as bad as the chemical-laden pond water from an industry far away that I had tasted long ago. That taste holds the title for the worst I've ever experienced, followed closely by today's breakfast and then the white creatures. I'm not sure what they were, but something is better than nothing, right? It gave me enough energy."

Based on the aroma emanating from the food carts that brought Kargoor's food, Anabelle proposed,

"It could be chicken. The flavor you're experiencing might be due to it being raised on poultry farms."

Kargoor realized, "So that was the chicken you guys were talking about. Now I understand why you said that white creature tasted better than chicken. But no worries, tonight, the whole town is going to have a feast better than chicken."

Anabelle complimented, "I admire your confidence."

Kargoor pondered, "Confidence is indeed a crucial feeling to possess, especially in times like these."

Anabelle softly nodded in agreement, then inquired, "Could you share more about this world?"

Taking a deep breath through his large nostrils, Kargoor began, "Where should I start? Should I begin from a time when magical creatures and humans lived harmoniously, forging an unbreakable bond that led to creatures sharing their magical gifts with humans? Or perhaps from the moment humans grew greedy, venturing down a dark path to harness the power of magical creatures into different crowns? Or maybe from the time darkness consumed people's hearts, that led to a war between people and creatures, and we had to fight to bring it under control?"

Anabelle countered, "No more talks about fights or sadness. Let's focus on love and beauty."

Kargoor replied, "I understand your desire to hear about the love and beauty of this world. But as you just mentioned love, my thoughts are consumed by her. Not to mention that she was not my first love, in which I had been lost, which clouded my eyes and stood as the reason for my being in this condition. She was my love and that is worth dying for. There were times when I wished for death to escape this form and return to where I came from. However, now I have a glimmer of hope. I can see her in my son. I eagerly anticipate looking after him, teaching him, and showing him the beauty of this world filled with love."

Anabelle softly smiled but got distracted by an unusual sound. Kargoor, recognizing the noise, wasted no time and sprinted toward its source. Anabelle spotted a Henosaur making the sound, though she had never heard that particular noise from it before. The creature continued its noise without any concern for its safety, seemingly prioritizing the sound even as Kargoor approached.

With incredible speed, Kargoor bit the neck and swiftly severed the head of the creature. It appeared to Anabelle as if Kargoor wielded the sharpest sword, slicing off the head in a mere moment.

Returning to his position, Kargoor instructed Anabelle, "Tell the others to be ready. The cry of that creature will bring the whole army of Henosaurs here in under thirty minutes."

Anabelle hurried to inform Ethan, finding Lily still asleep. Ethan and Anabelle stood there, uncertain of what to do near the hole in the wall. Anabelle proposed waking Lily to assist Kargoor, but Ethan had a different idea. He went to where the sword lay beside Lily, knelt, placed his hands on the sword, and said, "I hope the time has come."

Ethan attempted to lift the sword, but his efforts proved futile. Frustrated, he mumbled, "What am I doing wrong? It's hard to believe in myself if such things keep happening."

Lily remained undisturbed in her deep sleep. Anabelle, sensing Ethan's distress, wanted to console him. She sat beside him, searching for words to offer comfort. Before she could speak, Ethan abruptly got up and left the skull. Anabelle wished to assist him, silently uttering to the universe, "We need all the help we can get to stay strong. Why is this happening to Ethan? Don't you think he's ready yet? It's all because of this sword…"

She was abruptly shocked and unable to continue as she accidentally pushed the sword while speaking, and it unexpectedly moved. Doubting her eyes, she pushed it again for confirmation, and it responded. Trying to lift it, she found it surprisingly light, like picking up a feather.

Coming out of the skull in a mixture of shock and rage, Emily caught Ethan's attention. He observed his sister walking angrily towards the hole in the wall, carrying the sword. Seeing her with the sword gave him relief. He also noticed her unusual walk, which was different from her usual self. She walked swiftly, swinging her arms wide and taking long steps, reminiscent of the rage she was in when he first found her with the sword.

Anabelle swiftly joined Kargoor at the wall. Upon seeing her, Kargoor remarked, "Oh, it's you. I was expecting Lily. Be careful with the sword, it could hurt me. I don't want to leave this planet without talking to my son."

Anabelle turned to Kargoor, her silence filling the air with tension. Her eyes locked onto his as if his words had struck a nerve, stirring feelings of anger within her. Kargoor pondered his earlier words, finding nothing offensive that could explain her apparent anger. Suddenly, the sound of breaking or moving trees reached them. Anabelle, without a word, sprinted toward the source.

The movement of trees heralded the arrival of four Henosaurs advancing toward the hole. Anabelle dashed towards them, leaping high into the air when she was near the first creature. The sword's blade ignited in flames as she descended, effortlessly slicing through the creature's neck. Landing on the fallen creature's back, she swiftly moved to the second, piercing the sword into its heart. Pulling the sword out, she ran, leaped even higher, and aimed the sword towards the third creature between its eyes. The third creature fell lifeless. Exhausted, Anabelle turned her attention to the fourth creature that was still a distance away from the first three.

She retrieved the sword from the head of the deceased creature, raising it triumphantly to the sky. Performing a graceful 360-degree rotation, she prepared for a slicing action aimed at the fourth creature charging toward her.

Executing the slicing action, her sword sent forth an arc of fire resembling lava. The creature, just meters away, opened its mouth to bite the fiery arc. As the fiery arc approached, it evaporated the water from the creature's mouth, cooking its tongue. Upon contact, the arc sliced off the lower jaw, searing through the creature's brain. The jawless, brain-fried creature collapsed to the ground and slid toward her. Using her leg, she attempted to halt the creature, creating a visually impressive yet ineffective moment. Observing this, Kargoor's jaw dropped, marveling at her skills. He was relieved that she was an ally, acknowledging to himself that he would never want to face her in battle.

Kargoor muttered to himself, "Looks like I'll just be a spectator in this fight."

Anabelle swiftly dispatched each Henosaur that approached, but some managed to evade her only to meet their demise at Kargoor's formidable jaws. Despite Anabelle's growing fatigue, Kargoor, having rested, was just getting into the rhythm of the battle.

The fiery onslaught from Anabelle's sword quickly transformed the once-vibrant landscape into a charred wasteland. Assessing the increasing number of Henosaurs, Kargoor acknowledged that facing them alone would have been overwhelming.

Anabelle's weariness became apparent in her diminished speed and force. As the relentless stream of white creatures converged on the hole, the once-green and brown surroundings became a chaotic mix of white and red, consumed by the spreading fire.

Amid the battle, Kargoor pondered the motives behind the Henosaurs' relentless assault, contemplating the deeper machinations of the darkness orchestrating their actions.

Meanwhile, at Dragoor's skull, Ethan, alerted by the sounds of the ongoing battle, roused Lily from her sleep. Lily's immediate concern was the sword, and Ethan proceeded to recount the events involving the sword and Emily's capriciousness.

Lily expressed, "Yeah, I kind of sensed that too. It felt as though I had been using the sword for quite a while. While practicing with the sword, my mind was aware of the sword, but my body was not. It seemed like my mind's actions weren't fully supported by my body."

Concerned, Ethan inquired, "What should we do now? Without a sword, you can't control or lift rocks to protect us. "If I could have wielded the sword, I would have stayed here to defend both of you. I don't know what came over Emily. She just grabbed the sword and marched toward the hole without saying a word. I hope Kargoor can keep her safe."

Lily asked, "Why? Do you want your sister to be in your protection? Do you think she is not strong enough to fight and take care of herself? Why, because she is a girl?"

Ethan understood that Lily had misinterpreted what he had said and clarified, "Asking a person not to go for a fight due to their gender is different from asking a person not to go for a fight due to care. What would you do? If you had a brother, would you send him to the hole for a fight?"

Lily realized the stupidity of her question. Considering her options, Lily asked, "Should I go join Emily and Kargoor at the wall in the fight?"

Ethan said, "Were you even listening? It's like my words just flew away in the air without reaching your ear. We don't even know how to use the sword. Did you learn to use and control the powers overnight?"

Lily clarified, "It's just something with the sword. I didn't need practice. As soon as I touched it, all the cells in my body just knew what to do. It did not feel like I was holding the sword for the first time. The level of confidence that it gave me… I am just unable to express it!"

She quickly recollected Margoor's words and said, "It felt like I had all the things I needed for doing what I intended to do. Maybe this is what Margoor tried to tell us with the swimming illustration that she gave. We already have what we need. Only that I haven't touched a sword in my life, but how did I know how to use it? I think I need to go to the hole."

Ethan observed Lily and questioned, "The Lily I knew would have asked if she could join the others in the safe hall. You sound like a different person now. And what's your plan at the hole without the sword?"

Lily explained, "Our lives are at stake. So, I thought it would be helpful if I joined Kargoor and Emily at the wall. If Emily could pass me the sword at timely intervals, we both could participate in the fight."

After a moment of silence, Ethan looked at Lily and said, "I'm not sure about you, but I feel like I should go join the other people back in the town."

Lily disagreed, stating, "No. If we were supposed to be with the others, we would have been directed to go there and not have received the food this morning."

There was a massive explosion, reminiscent of the one Ethan heard when he encountered Emily in Koodam for the first time. However, this time, the sound was much louder. Although they could not visually see the source, the intensity of the sound hinted at something colossal and ominous.

In a matter of seconds, the clamor of the approaching Henosaur grew nearer to Ethan and Lily. With uncertainty about Kargoor and Emily's fate on one side and the imminent danger of the white creatures on the other, they realized that even if they started running, their chances of survival were slim as they witnessed some of the creatures heading their way.

Lily earnestly prayed to the universe for help and guidance through the ordeal, while Ethan also beseeched the universe to save them and the entire town.

In response to their pleas, they heard footsteps approaching from behind. Ethan, fearing it might be some wild animal trying to attack him from behind, turned his head to look, only to see a person sprinting towards the Henosaurs with a sword in hand. Both watched in awe as a blond-haired boy ran past them.

Lily and Ethan looked at him with a question in their mind, "Who was he, and how did he get the sword?"

With swift precision, the boy caught the sword like a spear and hurled it at a white creature's neck, piercing the center. Coming to a halt, he raised his hand, and the sword was dislodged from the creature's neck, flying back into his grasp.

Witnessing the boy's remarkable abilities, Ethan and Lily were both amazed and spoke simultaneously.

Ethan suggested, "I guess he controls the air!"

Lily added, "I guess he must be Marcus!"

Their eyes met, and simultaneously, they both exclaimed.

Ethan exclaimed, "He could be Marcus!"

Lily exclaimed, "He could be controlling the air!"

As they pondered this possibility, the blond-haired boy indeed turned out to be Marcus. However, their assumption about air control proved to be inaccurate. Marcus's ability was tied to the sword, granting him control over water. The sword, upon striking the creature's neck, harnessed the water in its blood, forming a protective shield of water molecules around itself. The water adhered to the sword, which was how Marcus was able to get the sword to fly back into his hand. Marcus, taking advantage of the large creature's body, used it as a water source.

Remaining composed even as the Henosaurs approached, Marcus demonstrated his skill by creating a sharp piece of ice, which he launched at another creature, swiftly eliminating it. With each successful kill, he efficiently collected water from the fallen creatures, gradually increasing the size of his icy weapon.

He reached a point where maintaining the ice state of the collected water became challenging, bringing an end to his method of using ice to defeat the white creatures. Marcus now had to rely on water in its normal temperature form. Forming a massive ball of water, he struck the faces of the creatures with extensive force, making it difficult for them to breath, and rendering them unconscious. Moving swiftly around the fallen creatures, he efficiently slit their throats.

Advancing, Marcus caused the white creatures in his path to fall, steering his way toward the hole in the wall. As he approached, he noticed two holes in the wall with creatures entering through only one, on the right side. It was a newly created hole. Through the first hole on the left, he saw fire being emitted, obscuring his view of the ongoing events.

The influx of creatures through the second hole increased. Marcus raised his sword, generating a smaller amount of tiny icy needles from the water ball with the energy he had left in his body. Guiding the icy needles in a circular motion, he targeted the necks of the creatures, inflicting damage and tearing flesh. With each pass, the needle number grew, resulting in more effective kills.

Through a combination of these tactics, Marcus successfully eliminated all the creatures entering through the second hole. Stepping out of the wall, he surveyed the ground covered with the lifeless bodies of burned white creatures, creating a barbeque-like aroma. However, the situation called for urgency rather than feasting. Marcus observed Kargoor, now covered in blood from numerous bite wounds, shouting in pain and anger as he breathed fire on the remaining Henosaurs attempting to bite him.

Marcus glanced downward and observed a girl lying on the ground, covered in blood. Hurrying towards her, he recognized her as Anabelle. Panic momentarily gripped him, thinking she might be dead. Relief washed over him as he realized she was still breathing, though struggling. Without hesitation, he scooped her into his arms.

Kargoor, noticing Marcus, called out, "Hey boy! Where did you come from? Take her and get inside the wall."

Marcus swiftly carried Anabelle within the protective confines of the wall. Just as he was entering, a Henosaur lunged to bite him, but he skillfully evaded and made it inside the wall.

Out of sight from the Henosaur that was chasing Marcus, inside the wall, Marcus, and Anabelle found refuge.

Ethan and Lily had followed Marcus, venturing too close to the wall. The creature, following Marcus and Anabelle, stepped inside the wall. Standing four to five feet away, it saw Ethan and Lily and advanced towards them. Realizing their mistake, Ethan and Lily attempted to retreat, but Ethan stumbled and fell to the ground. Lily went in to lend help to Ethan.

With the creature closing in, poised to bite, Ethan, and Lily braced for the worst, closing their eyes. However, they were surprised to hear the creature clapping its mouth twice above them without delivering a bite.

Opening their eyes, they saw the creature's head being pulled backward as another creature, the one they had pursued the day before and believed to be Kargoor's son, bit the back of its neck and dragged it away.

Kargoor's son grappled fiercely with the white creature, struggling to bring it down. Meanwhile, Ethan and Lily expressed their gratitude for narrowly escaping the clutches of the massive animal. Ethan's attention was drawn to Emily lying near the wall, covered in blood. Tears blurred his vision as he rushed to his sister, finding solace in the realization that she was still breathing.

Anabelle, however, was completely drained of energy, utterly exhausted from the ordeal. Kargoor's son, having successfully dispatched the white creature, emerged from the wall and took up a defensive position near the second hole.

Outside the wall, Kargoor, with a piece of a white creature's flesh in his mouth, witnessed his son walking out of the wall. Time seemed to slow down, and he conjured up an energetic, uplifting tune, everything happening in his mind. Hindered by the ongoing battle, he could not call out to his son.

Amid the chaos, Kargoor's anger intensified as he saw a white creature bite his son's leg. At that moment, Kargoor lost awareness of his own identity and physical pain. He was fueled by fury. He unleashed his strength, attacking the Henosaurs with every part of his body, particularly utilizing his tail and legs. Noticing that his son struggled without using fire to his advantage, Kargoor resolved to turn the tide.

Kargoor's command echoed, "Try blowing fire into the mouths of these creatures. Burn their insides."

His son, somewhat uncertain, inquired, "I can do that?"

Kargoor, reflecting on his son's capabilities, thought, "Plenty to learn, my boy."

Attempting to breathe fire, Kargoor's son encountered difficulty, much to Kargoor's surprise. It dawned on him that his son couldn't produce flames.

While the two beasts continued relieving the souls of the Henosaurs, Lily ventured out of the wall, seeking the sword Anabelle had left in the heat of battle. Spotting the weapon lying between Kargoor and his son in the massacre arena, she struggled to reach it amid their constant movement.

Observing Lily's plight, Kargoor's son, using his leg, tossed the sword toward her. However, in the process, he lost balance as a Henosaur launched a surprise attack.

Kargoor urgently shouted to his son, "Eyes on your enemy."

Chapter 9

Face of Darkness

A Henosaur approached Kargoor's son, getting dangerously close to his neck. Kargoor, shouting in alarm, sprinted towards his son in an attempt to save him. Despite his efforts, he was too far away to reach his son in time. Unexpectedly, something emerged from below, striking the white creature on its chest and causing it to recoil. This unexpected savior turned out to be a large block of rock raised by Lily with the power of the sword.

Acknowledging Lily's intervention, Kargoor expressed his gratitude. The onslaught of the white creatures diminished as the trio of Kargoor, his son, and Lily effectively dealt with the remaining threats. Together, they stood amid the aftermath, surveying the lifeless bodies of the white creatures they had collectively vanquished.

Observing the fiery aftermath, Lily commented, "Lot of fire everywhere."

Kargoor, attributing most of the fire to Anabelle, explained, "She did something remarkable with her sword. See that brain-fried, jawless creature over there? If you witnessed what she did to it, your mind would have been blown."

Taking charge of guarding the two holes, Kargoor, and his son remained vigilant. Meanwhile, Lily returned inside the wall to check on Anabelle.

Ethan, having carried Anabelle away from the wall, left her under a tree and hurried to Dragoor's skull to retrieve the food basket.

While searching for it, he felt thirsty. Peering into the basket, he noticed it contained less food, which might not be enough for Emily to regain her strength. So he refrained from eating it. As he dashed back to Emily, he spotted a succulent pink fruit about half the size of an average orange. It looked juicy, so he plucked two and began eating them on the way. As expected, they provided enough water to quench his thirst. Their sweetness made him regret not having tasted them before.

Bringing the basket to Emily, he offered her some honey and bread, providing her with much-needed sustenance to regain her energy.

Emily consumed a substantial amount of food, enabling her to sit independently. Curious about the recent battle, she eagerly listened as Ethan provided details, expressing her joy upon learning that Marcus had come back and joined the fight. Anabelle suggested that she join Marcus in the fight at the wall. Despite Anabelle's eagerness to join the fray and support them, Ethan intervened, informing her that Lily had gone to provide additional help.

Lily eventually rejoined the group, offering an update on the ongoing battle. Anabelle, concerned about Marcus, inquired about his whereabouts. Lily, unable to locate Marcus during the fight, relayed this information to Anabelle. Fearing the worst, Anabelle's heart skipped a beat as she considered the possibility of Marcus's demise. Distraught, she turned away from Lily and Ethan's conversation, rushing towards the wall.

Once outside the wall, Anabelle frantically searched for Marcus, shouting, "Marcus, can you hear me?" To her surprise, Kargoor's son responded, "Yes, I can. Loud and clear."

The revelation left everyone in shock. Marcus addressed their astonishment, acknowledging their likely confusion. He jokingly added, "Some of you might even be thinking if I ate Marcus."

In response, Ethan promptly reassured, "No, I didn't think that."

Ethan became the focal point as everyone shifted their gaze toward him. Clearing his throat, he remarked, "I'm sorry. You please continue," diverting the attention from himself. Marcus seized the spotlight to share his story.

"I'll have to begin my flashback now. And please don't worry, it's not going to be long," Marcus assured. All eyes were fixed on him as he delved into his narrative.

"The earliest memory I have is of being alone in Koodam, unable to make friends, wandering the streets alone. I was not used to being loved and cared for. But when I received it from Anabelle, it felt nice. Despite experiencing love and inhabiting a human form, a primal part of me yearned to hunt and feed. Thus, occasionally, I found myself drawn to the vicinity near the lone tree where a large creature's skull is now laying, seeking out small animals to satisfy this urge. Occasionally, stray goats would wander into the area, providing an opportunity to engage in a semblance of hunting, indulging in a playful enactment of the hunt."

Ethan interjected, "That skull guy is called Dragoor. And your father was the one who killed and ate him."

Lily hushed Ethan, signaling Marcus to continue.

Marcus resumed, "I kept hearing a voice, which grew worse day by day. Sometimes, I would get unconscious and wake up in a different place."

Ethan leaned toward Lily, whispering, "It happens to me a lot. Especially in college after lunch. I close my eyes and when I open them, I am in another class."

Lily, sensing something amiss with Ethan, gave him a peculiar look but refrained from addressing it, eager to hear Marcus's story.

Marcus shared, "The next day after people began walking weirdly, something happened to me. I found myself in the middle of a crowded street. I closed my eyes, and when I opened them, I was in front of this hole in the wall. I didn't understand what was going on. Feeling uneasy, I tried to run away, but I heard the voice again—a female voice. It asked me to follow some directions, leading me out of the wall to a place at a higher altitude. It instructed me to sit there, claiming it was a special place."

Ethan whispered to Lily, "I am afraid of high altitudes." Lily paid no mind to his comment.

Marcus continued, "The voice told me about my history—about what had happened to me in the past. It narrated a story about God's son, who was sent to this planet in the form of a dinosaur to serve punishment for the mistake he made. Around two hundred and fifty years later, God sent an angel with a weapon forged from his blood to kill his son and free him from his dinosaur form. However, the angel neglected her duty. She fell in love with the beauty and nature of this world and decided to stay for a while. She met God's son, but instead of killing him, she fell in love with him. They both had the best time together for a couple of years and as a representation of their love, they even had a son. Their happiness grew until one day when a wish-giving luminous butterfly arrived, carrying some bad news."

Kargoor realized that when his father said 'DIE NO SOR,' he meant dinosaur, which is the name of the creature form he was currently in.

Ethan whispered to Lily, "Oooh. I had seen one such butterfly."

Lily whispered, "I know. I was there with you."

Marcus said, "The butterfly carries a gift for the souls that see it during its time as that luminous butterfly. The angel sent by God refused the gift and asked for a wish instead. She wished for her son to be in a safer place, protected and guided by angels in necessary times. The butterfly granted her wish but also bore heavy-hearted news—that the time given for the angel to spend on this planet was over, and she had to return by burning in the fire as her body was destined to be destroyed by fire.

As the angel stood hopelessly, the butterfly sent out a bright light into the sky and disappeared, burning the angel alive. God's son tried to save his wife by searching for water nearby. However, when he returned, he saw that his wife had already died, and his son was running towards his burning mother's corpse."

Kargoor said, "I still remember that day. I thought you had died along with your mother. I saw you fall into the fire, and minutes later, there were only ashes left. But how did you escape? And how are you still alive?"

Marcus said, “I do not have any memory of that day. But the voice told me that I was saved by another angel that night and taken care of. As the grandson of the leader of the Devarnams and the son of two superior beings, I live longer than most organisms in this world. The angels felt that I was in danger, so, as per my mother’s wish, they protected me all the time and kept me hidden from this world. The voice told me that I did not have the memory of my life outside the wall as I got into a fight with a creature and got my head injured, thereby losing my memory. The voice said that it was an angel too and every time I was in danger, an angel helped me in some form. So the angels performed some magic on me to transform me into this human form and brought me inside the wall to keep me safe.”

Ethan cried and said, “You said your story won’t be that long, but you did not mention anything about it being so emotional.”

Marcus said, “Oh, God. Ah, I mean, my grandfather. What happened to him?”

Lily said, “Not sure. But he has been acting weird like this since you began the flashback for no reason.”

Kargoor asked, “Hey, Ethan. Did you eat a juicy pink fruit by any chance?”

Ethan said, “No.”

Kargoor said, “Good. If he would have—”

Kargoor was interrupted by Ethan as he said, "I ate two." And he laughed. He continued, "Ohh, why are you all flying?"

Kargoor said, "Oh dear. That is not good. This is the effect of that pink fruit. It makes humans drowsy as it makes the brain less active. It is not permanent, he just needs to rest. The only thing he cannot get now."

Anabelle turned towards Marcus and asked, "But how did you turn into this monster-like creature?"

Marcus said, "I was taught how the magic works. All I did was…"

He was disturbed as they all heard some sound. It felt like the ground was vibrating a little, caused by a pack of Henosaurs coming towards the wall.

Kargoor asked Ethan and Anabelle to go inside the wall. However, as Ethan was not acting himself, Anabelle had to help Ethan get inside the wall.

Lily planned a strategy and raised the ground on the battlefield to make a maze in front of the wall. She first raised a semicircular wall around the two holes with a greater diameter. Then, she raised interior walls for the semicircular structure to make a maze. There were many entrances for the maze, all in the direction from where the white creatures were coming, and only one was near the wall where Kargoor's and Marcus's mouths were waiting.

She had created the maze because she wanted the Henosaurs to be trapped in it, and when they figured the way out, Kargoor and his son would be waiting for them.

Lily stood on top of the maze wall, looking at the white creatures, getting confused about the maze, causing them to fall, bite themselves, and kill each other. She thought to herself, “I was thinking of bringing Emily into the maze, but it seems she can rest for some time.”

After a while, it seemed like the creatures were all communicating with each other and trying to figure out the maze. It seemed like they were being guided or controlled by a higher intelligence. But even though they figured the way out, Kargoor and Marcus were readily waiting for them. As the white creatures had figured their way through the maze, Anabelle had to join the fight to make the fight easier for Kargoor and Marcus. Lily was tired from creating the maze and had to rest for a while, so she handed the sword to Anabelle.

Lily thought Anabelle would be staying on the top of the wall to kill the creatures with the sword. But as soon as she got the sword, she jumped right into the maze and began slaughtering the creatures. Before jumping into the maze, Lily saw the rage on Anabelle’s face, and her behavior seemed a bit different. She understood what Ethan meant when he was describing Anabelle when she was holding the sword.

Lily went near the wall, to stay back, and regain energy. Marcus saw Lily standing on top of the wall. He asked, "Lily, can't you just drop stones on these creatures and kill them? It would make our work easier."

Lily said, "Yeah, I could do that. But after lifting ten stones and dropping, I'll get tired, and I'll not be able to lift any more stones."

Marcus gave another suggestion, "Could you make the maze walls move dynamically? That way, the Henosaurs would get confused, and it would buy us more time to rest between fights."

Lily thought Marcus's suggestion was a good one. She said, "Yeah, I'll need less energy for that." Then, she noticed Marcus didn't have his sword with him. She thought his sword would be helpful for her in the fight. She shouted, "Where is your sword?"

Lily could not hear what Marcus was telling her amid the cries of two white creatures being burned by Kargoor. He tried conveying what he intended to say by mouthing the words and with hand gestures. But on the other end, she could not understand his facial expressions and hand gestures in his dinosaur form.

Before she could clarify her doubt, she heard Anabelle calling for her. Anabelle was standing in the center of the maze on top of the maze wall. Lily rushed towards her, thinking she might have lost her energy, but she did not. Anabelle saw Lily moving towards her, and both of them went to the semicircular end of the maze, farthest from the wall.

They saw the Henosaurs along with some small yellow creatures entering the maze. The small yellow creatures were about the size of a dog, only about knee height for humans. Those yellow creatures began climbing the maze using the pile of dead white creatures stacked against the wall of the maze.

Anabelle and Lily were about to run back to warn Kargoor and Marcus. Something caught their attention before they could head back. It was a big green creature, a bit bigger than the white creatures, walking towards the maze. A human-shaped structure fully covered in white cloth was standing on top of the green creature.

Lily and Anabelle hurried back to Kargoor and Marcus, sharing the information. Kargoor mentioned that the yellow creatures, known as the Wolftahs, would be challenging to deal with due to their smaller size and increased resistance to fire. He said that the green creature was Crockabill, a harmless, kind creature who happens to be an old friend of his. He had no insight into the purpose or nature of the white human-shaped creature on top of the green creature, suggesting it might be associated with the darkness.

Marcus inquired, "Darkness? But I thought she said that structure was looking white."

Kargoor replied, "So what?"

Marcus expressed, "I thought darkness meant it should be in black."

Kargoor explained, "My son, it has nothing to do with appearance or color. It is the thoughts and actions that make one bright or dark."

Lily suggested, "I guess it is the creature called Vangoork, mentioned by Margoor. We'll have to control this situation. We should think of some way to protect the town by not letting these Wolftahs inside the wall."

Marcus agreed.

Anabelle asked, "Can you raise this maze to a much higher height so that these small creatures cannot get down, and even if they did, gravity takes care of killing them?"

Lily responded, "I think I can. It is an excellent suggestion, by the way. If I can raise the walls higher, it hinders the Wolftahs from reaching the top of the maze. Even if they reached the top, it would be difficult to reach us from above the maze. They would be forced to come through the maze, buying us enough time. But I'm already exhausted. I am not sure if I can muster the strength to do it with the little energy remaining in my body. I might faint. But let me try."

Lily took the sword from Anabelle. She noticed Anabelle's face change from rage to fear, moments after she handed over the sword. Lily attempted to raise the height of the maze walls, but a massive explosion occurred at the maze's center, shattering it into countless tiny stones, and killing all the creatures inside.

After the dust settled a bit, Marcus stood up and searched for the others amid the debris. All he could see were scattered stones, unable to locate Kargoor, Anabelle, and Lily. While scanning, he noticed Crockabill advancing, accompanied by the white human-shaped figure. An angelic voice commanded in his head, "Take out the sword."

Before Marcus could react, his mind was enveloped in a void surrounded by darkness. Confused and disoriented, he heard the angelic voice again urging him to take out the sword.

Ethan hurried towards the hole, witnessing the destruction of the entire maze. Still feeling drowsy, he found Marcus standing amid the wreckage, breathing heavily with closed eyes. Ethan called out for Kargoor, Lily, and Emily but received no response. Unable to locate Kargoor's massive dinosaur form, Ethan's eyes welled up with tears.

Continuing to shout names and search, Ethan asked Marcus for help in moving some stones, but Marcus remained unresponsive. Climbing atop the stones, Ethan scanned the surroundings but couldn't find their whereabouts.

Ethan's hope of finding the others faded as he observed the white human-shaped creature on top of

Crockabill. Expecting Marcus to confront the green creature and prevent it from entering the wall, Ethan was disappointed when Marcus moved towards the wall instead. Despite Ethan's attempts to communicate, Marcus paid no attention and continued towards the hole in the wall.

Uncertain of what to do, Ethan noticed a sword protruding from a pile of stones. Driven by thoughts of his town and its people, he rushed to the sword, gripping it tightly and attempting to lift it. However, the sword was wedged between the rocks, resisting his efforts. Shouting in frustration, Ethan, realizing he could not lift the sword, fell to his knees, and the rocks beneath him began to shake.

Initially, Ethan anticipated the ground to split and engulf him along with the rocks on which he was standing. But Ethan's expectations were not met. Instead, a few of the stones beneath him shifted, and Kargoor emerged with the sword impaled on the right side of his chest. Exhausted and in excruciating pain, Kargoor, aware of his imminent demise, witnessed his son walking towards the wall, breaking his heart.

Kargoor knew that his son was being controlled by the darkness as he felt the same being tried on him. But as his mind and soul were strong, he was able to fight, not letting his body and mind be controlled by the darkness. Encouraging his son, Kargoor said, "Fight it, son. Gain control of yourself from the darkness."

Despite Lily and Anabelle being injured, Kargoor shielded them during the maze's collapse. Ethan tried to usher them to safety. Observing the sword embedded in Kargoor's chest, Lily exclaimed, "What have I done?"

Marcus, upon hearing Kargoor, abruptly turned back and sprinted towards him. Before Kargoor could stand, Marcus collided with him, driving the sword deeper into his chest. Kargoor fell to the ground, writhing in pain.

Before heading toward the town, Marcus opened his mouth and blew cold, dry air on Kargoor's chest. The cold air did not harm Kargoor due to the curse of his father. The sword that was penetrated into his body was given by Margoor and was not forged by his father, so it could not kill him. Both Kargoor and Ethan did not know this fact about that sword. However, the sword in his chest grew colder, causing intense pain. Unable to stand the pain, Kargoor turned sideways and called for Ethan's assistance. He asked Ethan to pull the sword out, but Ethan hesitated, fearing he might cause further harm. He feared that if he held the sword, the sword might become heavy and kill Kargoor by cutting through his heart.

Despite Ethan's reluctance, Emily and Lily encouraged him, urging him to believe in himself. Meanwhile, Marcus proceeded into the town, accompanied by the Wolftahs. Ethan closed his eyes and recalled a fragment of his father's words, boosting his confidence. His father had told him, "Only you can play the role of you in this world and nobody else can."

Empowered by this realization, Ethan understood that saving Kargoor might not be enough to face Marcus and the Wolftahs. As Lily and Anabelle could not continue the fight in their state, he had to be the one to help Kargoor stand against the darkness. With determination, he aimed to defeat the white creature on top of Crockabill. Recognizing that he was the last hope for the town, Ethan pulled the sword from Kargoor's body as he said, "How hard could it be than my math tests."

As he withdrew the sword, another sword emerged from Kargoor's right chest. Ethan fell backward on the ground due to inertia and did not notice the second sword flying through the air. He heard Kargoor say, "I am happy," as he pulled out the sword, unaware of the second sword's trajectory. Kargoor smiled at Ethan, saying, "Look after my son," as he knew that his time on Gardoon had come to an end.

Kargoor's body ignited in flames, prompting Ethan and the others to retreat to avoid the fire. Unintentionally, the airborne sword found its mark, piercing Ethan's right chest. In agony, Ethan cried out, and Lily witnessed the sword penetrating his chest.

What transpired next seemed unimaginable. Kargoor transformed into ashes within seconds.

In place of Ethan stood a colossal owl, leaving Lily utterly speechless. Anabelle, unaware of Ethan's fate, urged Lily to explain. While picking up the sword from the ground, Lily gestured towards the giant owl and uttered, "Ethan."

Initially thinking the owl had stepped on Ethan, Anabelle displayed sorrow on her face, indicating she did not comprehend Lily's explanation.

Lily clarified, "That owl is your brother!" Anabelle's eyes widened as she realized her brother had transformed, prompting her to ask, "How?"

Observing Ethan's change into a giant owl, Crockabill halted. Ethan sensed fear in the air and noticed the Wolftahs had stopped advancing toward the town. Instead, they were retracing their steps toward him.

Ethan remarked, "I can feel the fear in the Crockabill through the vibration of the wind brushing against its body."

The creature on top of Crockabill spoke, "I have searched for this town for years. It's just as the traveler Narad described: 'Follow the light and you will find power.' I can feel the presence of the power inside. No one can stop me once I have my hands on that power!" The creature raised its hand, launching a large ball of blue light toward Ethan.

Spreading his wings, Ethan flapped them, manipulating the wind around him, redirecting the blue ball to hit the wall between the two holes, creating a substantial opening in the wall.

Lily, captivated by Ethan's actions, remarked to Anabelle, "I'm starting to fall in love with your brother." Anabelle, trying to get answers, reminded Lily, "Hey, focus. You haven't answered my question yet."

Lily instructed Anabelle, "Pierce the sword on the right side of your chest." Anabelle, surprised, questioned, "Are you kidding me?"

Lily responded, "Nope. I can relate to what happened to Ethan and the hand gestures Marcus was trying to show me earlier. As Marcus was in his dinosaur form, I could not understand his hand gestures. But now I get it. Just pierce the right side of your chest with the sword."

Meanwhile, Ethan advanced toward the darkness. The darkness expressed confusion, saying, "But… I can control animals. Why can't I control you?"

Ethan explained, "It's because your dumb, dark brain does not know the difference between a bird and an animal."

But the actual reason why the darkness was unable to control Ethan was that his natural form was a human and he had transformed into an owl with magic. Thus the darkness could not control Ethan's mind, unlike Marcus whose natural form was a dinosaur and he used magic to transform into a human.

The darkness laughed menacingly, "I know how my death would occur. You are just single in count. The features of the one who would kill me as per the words of the big bright luminous butterfly do not match yours!"

Chapter 10

Win Death

Darker than the void of space, within a cave shrouded in impenetrable darkness, lay Vangoork. It was stretched out on the floor, its body turned to the side in an attempt to ease its gnawing hunger. It racked its brain, searching for a solution to its plight—to find a way to exist without the constant torment of starvation. Its deepest desire was for sustenance to appear at its fingertips whenever it wished, granting it control over its surroundings. But alas, reality was unforgiving.

Its humanoid form, devoid of fur and wrapped in pallid skin, boasted limbs longer than those of a human, offering no advantage in the struggle for survival. Its pitch-black eyes, while striking, allowed too much light to penetrate, impairing its vision in the glaring daylight. The only feature that bestowed upon it a semblance of survival prowess was the elongated, razor-sharp nail that extended from its fingers, capable of carving deep gouges into tree barks with ease. Indeed, its appearance was the stuff of nightmares, capable of haunting the slumber of any unwitting observer.

As it crouched further, attempting to quell the relentless pangs of hunger, it felt its body teetering on the brink of collapse from days of starvation. The unforgiving weather outside the cave threatened to drain the meager warmth left within it, leaving it utterly devoid of energy. It lay there, helpless and resigned, its breaths dwindling, its existence hanging by a thread.

It closed its eyes, sensing the warmth slowly seeping away from its body. Reality began to blur around it, but amid the fading light, a glimmer of hope flickered within it. Despite the odds stacked against it, a sense of optimism stirred deep within its soul—a hope for a second chance, for redemption, for a better life. With determination, it made a silent vow to itself, promising to make a difference.

As it hunched over, desperate to alleviate its agony, a faint sound reached its ears—a sound that, under normal circumstances, would have brought it no joy. Yet, at that moment, it felt like a victory. Summoning every ounce of strength left in its body, it crawled toward the rat that had ventured into the cave, trembling with cold and seeking refuge. With newfound energy coursing through it, Vangoork seized the opportunity, feasting on the unexpected meal that would sustain him through the frigid night.

Not a day passed without Vangoork pondering the mystery of its existence, questioning why it was the sole unique creature on the entire planet and how it came to be. As it replayed the events of the previous night in its mind, one thing became abundantly clear—it could not endure another night in its desolate cave. After forty days of sheltering within its confines, it knew it was time to move on. Despite its frustration and dwindling energy, it trudged toward a nearby river, determined to find sustenance and forge a new path forward.

Due to its frailty and inherent weakness, Vangoork preferred to hunt under the cover of night, where he stood a chance against predators. Yet, as its situation grew dire, each day became a struggle for survival, with the looming threat of not seeing another dawn. Suddenly, its worst fear materialized as it found itself being pursued by a male lion.

Racing against death, it fled for its life, managing to scramble up a tree just in time. However, not before the lion left its mark, a deep scratch on its back that left it bleeding profusely. In a brief but fierce altercation that lasted mere seconds, Vangoork retaliated, leaving a scar between the lion's eyes with his razor-sharp nails. After a tense wait, ensuring the lion had departed, it descended from the tree and made its way to the river, drained of energy.

Arriving at the river's edge, Vangoork drank deeply, revitalizing its dwindling strength. Concealing itself in the safety of a tree above ground level, it lay in wait, hidden from the creatures that came to quench their thirst. Knowing its limitations, it avoided confrontation with larger animals and carnivores, acutely aware of its vulnerability in its weakened state.

Its vigil was rewarded as it spotted a deer approaching the river to drink. Positioned too far away to strike, it hesitated, knowing the fleet-footed creature could easily outpace it. As the deer prepared to depart, Vangoork readied itself to pounce, poised to unleash its sharpened nails upon its unsuspecting form. Yet, before it could make its move, the deer bolted at the unfamiliar sound of a creature from a distant waterfall, eluding its grasp once again.

With its hunger unsatiated and desperation setting in, Vangoork's attention was drawn to the distant rumble of the creature near the waterfall. Intrigued by the unfamiliar sound, it felt compelled to investigate, hoping it might lead it to some form of sustenance.

Upon reaching the waterfall, exhaustion washed over it, and it lamented its decision to journey so far, draining what little energy it had. Regret gnawed at it, questioning if it should have remained hidden, waiting for potential prey to come to it.

Yet, this thought proved misguided. Had it stayed concealed in the tree, it would have faced a bleak fate, for the creatures drawn to the water were deterred by the unsettling sounds emitted by the mysterious newcomer.

Its focus was abruptly seized by an extraordinary sight—a black dragon reclining near the falls. Though Vangoork had never encountered such a creature before, its presence was unmistakable.

The dragon's appearance was nothing short of majestic. Its colossal form, adorned in scales as dark as the night sky, gleamed faintly in the dim light. Its wings, vast and sinewy, resembled a shroud of darkness, poised for swift and agile flight. Each beat of its wings echoed like distant thunder, resonating through the air. Yet, amid its shadowy exterior, its eyes blazed with a fiery crimson glow, illuminating the darkness with an intensity that belied its serenity. Though one horn was missing, the other remained sharp and menacing, surpassing even Vangoork's sharpened fingernails in deadliness.

The dragon rose to its feet, its gaze fixed on the cascading water. It quenched its thirst before exhaling wisps of smoke with each breath. Vigilant, it scanned its surroundings for any signs of danger, then settled back down, favoring its injured left leg.

Vangoork, shrouded in darkness, observed from afar, its attention drawn to the sword embedded in the dragon's chest, a wound still seeping blood. The scent of the dragon's blood tantalized its senses, igniting an insatiable thirst that rivaled even that of vampires.

Aware of the dragon's weakened state, Vangoork yearned for its demise, envisioning a feast upon its flesh. However, its plans were interrupted by the arrival of a majestic golden dragon, radiant against the backdrop of the falls. The black dragon rose to meet its golden counterpart, the two entwining their necks in a display of affection. Vangoork discerned the bond between them, realizing they were lovers.

As the golden dragon attempted to remove the sword from the black dragon's chest, the injured creature restrained it, communicating in the ancient language of dragons. Eventually, the golden dragon departed through the waterfalls, leaving as swiftly as it had arrived.

Driven by its thirst for blood, Vangoork plotted to exploit the dragon's vulnerability. Yet, before it could act, a colossal gorilla, equal in size to the dragon, emerged from the waterfalls and swiftly dispatched the wounded creature. With a triumphant roar, the gorilla claimed victory before vanishing into the waterfalls once more.

Vangoork seized the opportunity to sate its hunger, descending upon the dragon's neck with fervor. The supple flesh yielded easily to its bite, and it feasted until its senses returned, prompting it to ponder the origin of these mysterious creatures. Despite its efforts to uncover their source at the waterfall, all he found was an impenetrable rock shrouded in opacity.

Turning its attention to the gleaming sword embedded in the dragon's heart, Vangoork approached cautiously. As it attempted to retrieve the weapon, rustling in the nearby bushes startled him, though it found no source for the disturbance. Suddenly, an unpleasant aroma invaded its nostrils. Eager to distance itself from the fallen dragon, it withdrew the sword, triggering a sudden conflagration that reduced the creature to ash, save for its head—a consequence of Vangoork's earlier feast upon its neck.

Grateful for its unwitting foresight, Vangoork claimed the sword and made its way back to its cave. En route, it was unsettled by the resounding roar of an unfamiliar beast, sending tremors through its body. Though far from the site of the fallen black dragon, it recognized the mournful cry of the golden dragon, lamenting the loss of its companion.

Vangoork neared its cave, casting a glance back at the waterfall ablaze in dragon fire. Even from its vantage point, the inferno appeared vivid and intense, hinting at the devastation wrought by the dragon's wrath. It couldn't discern the fate of the waterfall's waters, but he surmised they had likely evaporated under the dragon's fury.

As it pondered the spectacle, its attention was drawn to shimmering, luminous tiny butterflies fluttering nearby. Entranced, it followed the trail of these ethereal creatures back to a pulsating tree from which they emanated. To its bewilderment, the tree began to swell and transform until it revealed the form of a colossal luminous butterfly, Margoor.

Startled by the unexpected transformation, Vangoork braced himself, fearing the butterfly's intent. However, Margoor reassured it of her benign nature and explained her purpose: to converse with it.

As they spoke, Vangoork's thoughts turned to the magical beings it had encountered—the two dragons and a gorilla. Margoor elucidated that they hailed from another world, traversing through a secret magical passage accessible only to bearers of the soul stone. As Vangoork grappled with the implications of this revelation, Margoor delivered the unsettling news of its impending demise.

She said,

"*Without fulfilling your purpose*

Watching a Thousand Eyes

Freed by multiple colors

Yet, they end up in the dark

Only follow the light, and you

From darkness, shall come to light"

With those words, Margoor transformed into a tiny insect, emanating a brilliant light that nearly blinded Vangoork. Stunned by Margoor's revelation, it struggled to recall her exact message, but the sense of impending doom lingered—a foreboding warning of being hunted by creatures of various hues.

From that fateful night onward, sleep eluded it. Driven by a desperate will to survive, it descended into darkness, committing unspeakable acts. Its relentless hunt targeted any creature adorned with multiple colors, its twisted logic dictating their demise. Years passed in a relentless cycle of slaughter until a startling revelation dawned upon it: an innate ability to sense and command the creatures around it, an ability of the sword it was holding onto. Exploiting this newfound power, it coerced them into forming a formidable army of Henosaurs, manipulating them to multiply and bolster its forces.

Half a century passed, culminating in the eve of the Call of Dream—a pivotal moment for Vangoork. Encountering a majestic peacock, a long-forgotten notion resurfaced in his mind. The peacock, with its vibrant plumage and myriad eyes, symbolized the epitome of multicolored creatures. Swiftly, it dispatched its white army to eradicate every peacock from existence, finding solace in the belief that it had exterminated them all.

Vangoork stood in the battleground, facing a giant owl, without knowing the meaning of fear, determined to acquire the power that lies within the wall. Yet, as it stood facing Ethan in his towering owl form, a chilling realization dawned upon it—the consequences of its actions now looming before it.

It saw a giant peacock emerging behind the giant owl, realizing its predicament. The peacock, its doom, spread its feathers, capturing its vision. The thousand eyes on the peacock's feathers looked at it. It felt like all the souls that it had killed ruthlessly were staring at it in rage as the peacock transformed into fire, including its feathers. Faced with this spectacle, Vangoork attempted to retreat, losing control of Crockabill on which it was standing, which dropped it to the ground and fled in fear.

Ethan and Emily approached Vangoork in their colossal being form, and as they looked down on it, it retrieved its sword tied to its back, like the ones inside their chest, which granted it the ability to control animals. Emily breathed fire, and Vangoork along with its dark intentions turned into ashes, leaving the indestructible sword alone on the ground.

Neither of them noticed the dagger with a yellow crystal on its hilt that had emerged from Vangoork's body. But it was hidden beneath its bones and ashes.

Emily expressed, "Nothing can escape the purest element." Ethan, gazing at the peacock, inquired, "Emily, is that you?" With a smile, Emily confirmed, "Yes, brother. I am the same Emily whom you had lost when you were young."

Curious, Ethan asked, "I was waiting for this moment. I knew for sure that you were my sister. You were the one not accepting it. What made you realize the truth?"

Emily explained, "I just realized the moment I saw your wings. I knew I was your sister."

Ethan, puzzled, exclaimed, "Oh… Wait. What? My feather. How?"

Emily chuckled and said, "I am just kidding. It felt like some kind of barrier that was hindering me from remembering my childhood days. As soon as I transformed into this peacock, that barrier was released. And I felt like I was being angry at everything I saw when I was holding onto the sword. But now, as the threat is gone, my anger has also reduced. I do not recollect having any problems with this terrifying white humanoid creature. But it felt good, as if I got my revenge for something it had done to me. I feel victorious after I incinerated it."

As Emily's anger subsided, the flames around her body vanished. Her feathers still emitted fire, though not as intensely.

Ethan asked, "How did you escape from the Nivara River? I saw the river sweep you away with its strong current. It couldn't have been possible for anyone, especially a young child, to escape."

Emily remembered, "When I fell, I drank a lot of water and passed out quickly. Then, I recall laying on my back on solid ground and a woman with long blonde hair, around forty years old, giving me mouth-to-mouth to clear my lungs. I was in pain and couldn't see clearly, but I felt safe and fell asleep. When I woke up, I was with my foster parents, who took great care of me. After the near-death experience, I couldn't remember my life before the river. I couldn't recall my real parents, but I felt I had a big brother who cared for me. I asked my foster parents about you, but they always denied it. Maybe they didn't want to miss seeing Emily's enchanting smile."

Ethan grinned, saying, "I can't describe how happy I am." Emily smiled back, touching her peacock's head against Ethan's owl beak.

Curious, Emily inquired, "So what is it? What are your sword's superpowers?"

Ethan shared, "I guess it's controlling air." Emily responded, "Cool."

Ethan elaborated, "I can feel the changes in the air around us."

Emily, nodding her peacock head, exclaimed, "Awesome."

Ethan continued, "I am feeling the air molecules near you expanding and moving towards the sky."

Confused, Emily asked, "What?"

Ethan explained, "The threat is gone. You can bring down your fire in your feathers."

Emily apologized, "Oh. Oh, sorry, didn't realize I had feathers."

As she brought down the fire, curious about Emily's feathered peacock form, Ethan asked, "But how do you have feathers?"

Playfully, Emily replied, "Why are you asking? Do you feel jealous since you do not have such beautiful feathers like mine?"

Ethan smiled and reminisced, "I just remembered a similar fight we had when we were kids. But I was not asking in jealousy. I asked because only male peacocks have feathers, but you are a girl. So why do you have feathers."

Emily doubtfully asked, "How did my body change gender?"

Their conversation was interrupted by a faint voice calling their names. It was Lily. She was shouting at them, asking them to convert to their human form. Emily immediately took the sword out of her chest with her mouth and converted to her human form.

Lily saw Emily and said, "I think I should give you some privacy."

Realizing her lack of clothing, Emily swiftly inserted the sword back and transformed into a peacock. In her peacock form, she observed her brother in his owl form bending down and investigating the lower part of his body.

Ethan gazed up at his sister and remarked, "I don't think I have my thing."

Confused, Emily inquired, "What thing?"

Ethan clarified, "The thing I should be having as a boy."

Emily looked at Ethan without saying anything. Wondering why Emily transformed back into a peacock, Ethan questioned, "Why did you convert back into a peacock?"

Emily explained, "Do you remember the clothes we were wearing?" Realizing, Ethan whispered, "Oh no… I am not wearing anything."

Concerned about Lily below, Ethan said, "Thank God I was checking for my thing and did not convert back into my human form. I could have stunned Lily."

Emily reassured, "She is already stunned. But the good news is, my injuries from the fight have disappeared."

Ethan said, "Oohh. Don't worry. She is family."

Lily shouted from the ground, "You guys know that your voices are loud, and I can hear them, right?!"

Ethan considered asking Lily for help in bringing them some clothes, but before he could, both he and Emily were captivated by the appearance of a majestic white elephant with very long tusks. Overwhelmed, Ethan was shaking and had goosebumps at the sight of Lily as an elephant.

Emily expressed, "Wow. I have never seen a white elephant before."

Lily, surprised, asked, "I am an elephant?"

Both Ethan and Emily nodded their heads. Lily took a few steps back, started rotating her head, and began playing around with her trunk. She raised her trunk in excitement and wanted to touch Ethan's head. However, she didn't realize how heavy her trunk would be for an owl and accidentally dropped it on Ethan's head, causing him to fall to the ground. Lily apologized to Ethan, explaining that she just wanted to touch his head and did not mean to hurt him. Ethan stood up and stared at Lily.

To change the topic, Lily asked, "I have heard owls struggle to see in the daylight. How can you see?"

Ethan explained, "Yeah, I had that doubt too. I heard that owls' pupils do not get smaller like humans to block the sunlight, so they often close their eyes halfway or more in daylight. But my pupils seem to be able to get smaller and bigger like humans."

Emily remarked, "So you are like an evolved owl with human eyes." Ethan replied, "Maybe."

Marcus, in his dinosaur form, came running towards them. At first, he thought the owl, the peacock, and the elephant posed a huge threat to the towns. However, as he approached, he heard them speaking and realized they had used the sword's magic to transform into their colossal forms. Excited, he said, "Wait, let me guess." He looked at the white elephant and said, "Ethan?"

Lily shook her head and corrected, "It's Lily."

Emily smiled softly and commented, "I bet." Before she could finish, Marcus looked at the peacock and confidently said, "Ethan."

Emily replied, "I was about to say, I bet you would be wrong in this attempt. And I was right. It's Emily."

Marcus then looked at the owl and complimented, "You have beautiful eyes. I would have never guessed this owl form as Ethan."

Ethan agreed, "Yeah, I know. It just happened. I heard you."

Marcus observed, "So we are all in male animal form?"

Ethan requested, "Please stop pouring oil into a burning fire. I am the only odd one here."

Marcus humorously lamented, "Ohh. You do not have company. (sighed) I wish I were a female dinosaur."

Ethan asked, "So that you can give me company?"

Marcus clarified, "No. So that I could have beautiful eyes."

Emily questioned, "So you mean to say my eyes aren't beautiful?"

Marcus reassured, "Your peacock eyes and Ethan's owl eyes are nothing compared to your human eyes."

Emily blushed and said, "Really?" Marcus replied, "Hundred percent."

Ethan jokingly warned, "Please do not kiss in this form. It would be a horror scene. Oh, they are kissing. And I was right." Ethan turned towards Lily and saw a bright light behind her head. Ethan was looking at that light, mesmerized.

Lily was in shock, thinking Ethan was looking at her, and panicked, "I am not going to kiss you."

Ethan clarified, "What is that?"

Lily said, "What do you mean? We haven't kissed before. And I do not want my first kiss from an owl."

Ethan explained, "That light. Where is it coming from?" Lily realized that Ethan did not mean to kiss her, and she immediately turned back to escape the awkwardness. The four were looking at a bright light. Lily said, "Margoor?"

Chapter 11

Nilamaaru

The four, in their huge animal forms, were looking at the bright light. Lily's assumption was not correct, as the bright light did not resemble a luminous butterfly. As they were looking at the light curiously, a voice spoke, "Greetings, Warriors. I am Oli. I come from the soul dimension, bearing some information.

This is not the end. It is, in fact, the beginning of a far greater danger lurking out there. Darkness has engulfed the hearts and minds of many living beings in this world. Mandrook and Koodam have been under the protection of magic for a reason. The magic wall was built to guard something very powerful inside. Now that the magic wall is broken, darkness will come in search of that power. Always keep an eye out for something dangerous. All that looks good is not good, and all that looks dangerous is not dangerous.

The final message – 'Nilamaaru'."

Having said that, Oli disappeared.

Ethan asked, "What was that? I thought it was all over."

Emily said, "You thought the wall was there only to protect us from the darkness?"

Ethan said, "Yeah. What could be worse than the darkness with a magic sword controlling animals?"

Marcus said, "Guys. You all have not traveled out of this wall much. But I have. This world must be big. By big, I mean very, very big."

Lily said, "Guess it's time for us to explore the world and prepare ourselves if we have to face any danger."

Ethan said, "Oh gosh. I can't read the whole library."

Emily said, "What happened to the yellow doggy creature?"

Marcus said, "Don't worry about them. I took care of them."

Marcus thought the others would continue with something else, but they wanted to know how he was so sure about the Wolftahs. He realized that as he saw the others not talking and began speaking, "During the fight, I lost consciousness. It felt like I was in a dream. Everything that was happening in my dream was good and sweet. I felt very happy in my dream. But there was a voice that was continuously telling me to take the sword out. As soon as I got distracted by that voice, my dream switched. I did not realize back then that I was in a dream, but now I get it. I must have been in like fifty different dreams within fifty steps I took inside the wall. At some point, I realized that the voice belonged to an angel who was trying to help me gain my consciousness back. After a great struggle with Vangoork in my mind, I took out the sword from my chest to transform into a human. That is when I broke out from the control of the darkness."

Emily asked, "Was it very difficult for you to break loose from the control of Vangoork?"

Marcus said, "Not sure how exactly. But I guess it was not all me. There was a moment when Vangoork lost control of my mind. That is when I was able to take out the sword and transform into a human. After I transformed, I saw the Wolftahs running back towards the wall. But within a few minutes, the creatures lay down on the ground and did not do anything dangerous. They were afraid of seeing me as a human, so they communicated with each other and ran out of the wall.

It was like they were being called back by Vangoork, but suddenly, it lost control over the Wolftahs. I stopped hearing the angry voice that I used to hear. I feared converting back into my dinosaur form as I might get under Vangoork's control again. So, I sprinted towards the hole and when I came near the wall, I saw a giant owl and a peacock. I knew I could not go against a colossal owl and a peacock, so I inserted the sword in my chest to take my original form."

As he was recounting the incident, he had just remembered about his father. He asked, "Where is my dad?"

The three remained silent for a couple of minutes, and Emily said, "Your Dad is in a happier place. A place where he wanted to go from the moment your mother died but decided not to go the moment he learned that you were alive. He yearned to show you this world and teach you his ways. He wished to have spent more time with you. But things did not turn out the way he wished. The mighty Kargoor fell at the hands of the darkness. He died peacefully, saying he was happy as he let out his final breath. Though I am not sure if he'll visit our world during your time here, I am pretty sure that he'll always be concerned about you and will constantly be watching over you."

As Marcus heard about the death of his father, tears began welling up in his eyes. He felt the sudden change in the clouds above him as he could sense the water in the clouds move. He looked up as the rain poured down. He asked Ethan, "Did you feel that? The sudden change in the clouds? After all, the clouds are made up of air and water, right? It's like my father is watching me and does not want me to be seen crying. I feel like he is trying to wipe my tears by causing the rain."

Ethan nodded, agreeing that he was able to sense the movement of the clouds. He said, "It's just like when your father cried. The sky poured down in a similar way to wipe away his tears. He was so worried that he had lost you when you were young. But when he learned that you were alive, he was the happiest soul in this whole world. However, moments later, it was Lily who was the happiest soul in this world as she got hold of her sword."

Marcus said, "I just learned that my father is still alive. I thought I did not have a bond with him, so it would not hurt much. But it makes me sad. I hope I have the strength to overcome this pain soon."

Emily wanted to change the topic of discussion, so she asked, "Speaking of swords. Were you born with the sword inside you?"

Marcus did not speak as he was not sure. But it did help him overcome the sadness.

Lily said, "Seems like most of these swords came from a colossal being. Emily's sword came from the blue creature, Sourtail, that she killed. That was the first sword the three of us saw. Ethan's sword came from Kargoor's body. Marcus's is his own, and we do not have any idea where my sword came from before the darkness took it."

Ethan just remembered something from the book he had read about swords. He said, "I read about the swords' powers in a book. But that book said that the swords had powers like creating and controlling fire, controlling air, controlling animals, and others. I thought there were different swords with different powers. But during the fight, the same sword that gave Emily the power to create and control fire gave Lily the ability to control rocks."

Emily asked, "So all swords possess the same capability, but their powers vary with different people, is it?"

Ethan said, "Seems like it."

Lily asked Ethan, "How did you overcome your drowsiness?"

Ethan said, "Oh, that. I am pretty sure that I dozed off for a bit. I even had a dream about talking to a person in the mist. I don't know who that person was, I could not see his face properly. But he was talking about me being an incarnation of him to protect their worlds from destruction.

He said sadness will hover upon my back, not to hold me back, but to make me strong. He mentioned that, similar to me, there are other incarnations of him, living in other worlds in our Kan universe, and if required, we'll meet. He warned me not to doubt myself as I was attracting negative energy towards myself by doubting my capabilities. He said that is how Vangoork found our town's existence and launched the first attack on our wall, creating the hole from a very faraway place.

My dreams are getting weirder day by day and my fear increases with each one (sighs). So, that is how I overcame the drowsiness. But I have to say that after that sleep, I felt like my body had gained enormous energy.

My muscles felt strong. It was like my muscles did a workout when I was asleep. It gave me confidence and I guess it could be one reason why I was able to lift the sword."

Emily asked, "What do you all feel about the last message Oli gave us? What do you think it means? I haven't heard that word 'Nilamaaru' before."

As soon as Emily completed her sentence, she disappeared. The three looked at each other in shock.

Ethan said, "I just got my sister back! I don't want to lose her again!"

From the ground, Emily shouted, "I guess it is the transformation word. I am back in my human form."

Ethan had a sense of relief to know his sister did not disappear. But he suddenly realized that she did not have any clothes on her. He rushed to cover Marcus's mouth with his feather hand and asked Lily to catch hold of Marcus's hands with her trunk to stop him from uttering the words given by Oli.

Emily again transformed back into the peacock and saw both Ethan and Lily catching Marcus. She asked them both what they were doing. Ethan said, "Nothing. I was just checking the sharpness of Marcus's teeth. He has at least fifty teeth in his mouth and are stinking like chicken blood."

Emily said, “I know why you both were catching Marcus. But there is no need to worry. After I said that word, I changed back to my human form with the sword in my hand, and I was wearing some clothes.”

Ethan said, “Really?”

Ethan did not want to take the risk, so he wanted to test it out first. He said, “Nilamaaru.” He changed back into his human form and shouted from the ground, “It is awesome! I have a knight’s armor.”

The others said the magic word and transformed back into their human forms, each with their sword in their hand. When they were about to return, they saw four bicycles parked at the opening of the wall.

On their way back home, Marcus asked if someone could fill in on the events that happened after the maze collapsed. Emily volunteered and narrated the incidents, excluded the part about Marcus fighting Kargoor and Ethan taking the sword out of Kargoor. She thought Marcus might blame himself for his father’s death and might be angry at Ethan for pulling the sword that killed his father.

The dagger from Vangoork’s body lay there, waiting for it to be discovered. Its destiny was far greater than simply being inside Vangoork’s chest.

Chapter 12

Calm After the Storm

Forty-three days later.

The Call of Dream had not yet ended. The pets were still in Koodam and people were still walking around with their hands raised. The frequency of the four of them meeting together was reduced. Ethan asked Emily to come stay with her actual parents in their house, but Emily refused, saying that she respects her foster parents who took care of her and raised her, and that she wishes to be beside them for their needs. Lily's visits to Ethan also were reduced as she was worried about her mother's health and wanted to spend time with her.

Due to these situations, Ethan reduced the time he spent outdoors. So he brought some books to his house to do his research on magic and the sword.

Spending time in isolation began affecting his mind. He would often go to the marvelous place to sit inside Dragoor's skull and think of the fight that happened between him and Marcus two weeks back.

After the fight with darkness, the four decided to step out of the wall to cover some area in pairs, taking turns. They decided to do this to figure out if there could be anything that could affect their town and to get some idea about how big their world was.

They decided that Marcus and Ethan would go out while Lily and Emily stayed back in the town for protection, as Lily's rock control power was best for defending their towns, and Emily's fire control power was best for attacking the enemies. One day, while outside the wall, the two got into a disagreement, and Ethan called Marcus a monster and revealed the fact that he was the reason that his father fell on the ground and got hurt.

When they returned, Emily did not like her brother calling Marcus a monster and was angry at him as he had revealed the information that she had kept a secret from Marcus. However, as Ethan did not apologize to Marcus, Emily and Marcus stopped visiting Ethan. Lily tried to console Ethan, but he was not in the mood to listen to anyone.

After reflecting on the fight for some time, he hopped on his bicycle. While riding back home, he saw a swarm of bees collecting honey from flowers. Intrigued, he followed the bees, and they led him to the bridge on his way to college. Standing there, he gazed at the crystal clear water of the river, Nivara, under the bridge, a sight he had always dreamed of. He blamed himself for not noticing it sooner. The clean water eased the pain in his mind.

From behind, he heard Lily's voice, "Your ego hasn't left you yet, has it?" Ethan turned to find Lily. He replied, "Whatever pain I might be in, your eyes make them vanish."

Lily walked over to stand beside him, also admiring the water. She was not as surprised as Ethan, having seen the water a few days back. She said, "This place is special. Whenever I come here, I feel a sense of peace."

Ethan asked, "Remember the day you were asking for volunteers to save the environment, and I volunteered first?" Lily nodded.

Ethan shared, "I volunteered first because that day, while riding to college, my cycle chain broke right here. I saw the dirty river and felt I should do something about it. On that day, my thoughts were all about talking to you and about making the environment better. Now the environment is cleaner, and I talk to you without fear. But my heart isn't in a good state. Since my sister stopped visiting, I have not been myself. I tried building the courage to talk to Marcus and Emily, to ask them to scold me, hit me, and do whatever they wanted to erase their anger about my actions. But I'm no better. I'm just a coward who can't accept his mistake and apologize."

Lily gently placed her hands on Ethan's shoulder and reassured him, "Nobody is perfect in this world. Nobody is always happy or sad. How good would it be if we always had sweets? It becomes boring over time, right? We need some sourness, bitterness, and spice from time to time to make life interesting. This sorrow will pass."

She gently wiped Ethan's tears and turned his face towards her. With compassion, she spoke, "The Ethan I know risked his life to defeat the darkness. Doesn't that sound courageous to you? Healing a wound, especially one created by words, is tough. But it doesn't mean it can't be healed. I believe in you. You'll sort things out by talking to your sister and Marcus. You've already taken the first step by accepting your mistake. Change is the only constant. Just give it time, and you'll gain clarity."

Lily's words brought calmness to Ethan's emotions, more than the clear water sight of Nivara could. He looked into Lily's eyes, and they both moved closer. Nervous, they closed their eyes, ready to kiss. However, someone abruptly pulled them away and turned them away from the river. To their surprise, their psychology professor stood before them.

Lily exclaimed, "How is this possible, Professor? How can you stand on two legs?"

Their professor looked at the two and smiled. He asked them to follow him with a hand gesture and walked towards his parked cycle, his hands raised.

Ethan remembered a similar event from his dream where he saw his professor standing on his own feet.

The two were stunned to see that their professor's condition had been suddenly cured. How could this be possible? They were left without answers, but their focus quickly shifted to something even more significant that was unfolding in their town.

The professor guided them to a safe hall in Mandrook, where people from their town were gathering. Lily questioned, "Is our town in danger again?"

Ethan pondered, "I guess so. But why are we directed to safety instead of the wall?"

Lily wondered, "What could this mean?"

Ethan questioned, "Do you think Emily and Marcus are safe? Could they be at the opening in the wall, fighting?"

Lily could not provide answers to Ethan's questions. Despite Ethan's attempts to go to the opening in the wall to check and find Emily and Marcus, he was stopped, and taken to a safe place. Both their families were there, and the entire town moved into a safe house with enough food and water to last for several days.

Confused, Ethan and Lily wondered why everyone was brought to safety and what they were running from. Inside the safety hall, everyone stood with raised hands. Lily speculated, "Could another creature engulfed in darkness be the reason for this chaos, and one of Kargoor's siblings is here to handle the situation?"

Before Ethan could respond, everyone lowered their hands and held onto each other with their hands. Ethan and Lily clung to each other, patiently waiting to understand the situation. The town fell into silence, devoid of pets that were still in Emily's town.

Suddenly, a terrifying sound filled the air, resembling roaring or thunder. The noise grew louder and more powerful, evoking a sense of impending danger. People tightened their grip on each other. Accompanied by crashing sounds, the wind intensified the terror.

Ethan pondered how their town could be saved from the source of the noise. Soon, they felt water at their feet. It was a tsunami, destroying parts of their town but fortunately not claiming any lives. Ethan and Lily, unfamiliar with tsunamis, were left bewildered by the unprecedented event.

After a few hours, the roaring sound subsided, and everyone exited the safety hall. The water had mostly receded, and the people began walking out of the safety halls with their hands raised.

Ethan and Lily could not find their bicycles due to the tsunami, but two people provided them with wet but rideable cycles. They quickly rode to Koodam to check on Emily and Marcus, discovering that their town was not significantly affected.

Ethan and Lily reached Emily's house, finding her sitting outside calmly. Emily remained furious with

Ethan, not interested in talking to him, offering only a greeting to Lily. When Lily narrated about the tsunami that almost engulfed their town and inquired about their part of the town's safety during the tsunami, Emily mentioned hearing a strange sound and that the water did not reach their town. The sound made her take out her sword, but as she observed the villagers continue with their usual activities, she put her sword away and resumed her tasks after the roaring sound ceased.

Concerned for Marcus, Ethan asked about his whereabouts. Emily questioned if Ethan intended to fight with Marcus again. Lily clarified that they were there to check on their well-being and not to start a fight. Emily mentioned Marcus had some work in Ethan's town and had left earlier. Ethan urgently asked when Marcus had gone.

Hearing about the situation at Mandrook, Emily was terrified. She was afraid that something bad might have happened to Marcus. When she was searching for her sword earlier, she figured that Marcus's sword was missing, so she assumed that Marcus would have taken his sword along with him. She did not say it out loud, but in the back of her mind, she doubted if Marcus was the one who caused the tsunami.

Emily mentioned, "Long back. It must be about two to three hours ago."

Ethan looked at Lily and said, "That is when the water hit our town."

The three of them hopped on their bicycles and rode towards Ethan's town, assuming Marcus might be outside the wall as they did not see him in Mandrook.

Upon reaching the spot where they first encountered Margoor, they were surprised to find that Dragoor's skull was missing. In its place, Marcus knelt, crying and gazing at a human-shaped figure floating in the air. As they rushed toward Marcus, the figure disappeared.

Chapter 13

Up We Go

Emily knelt beside Marcus, inquiring about what had happened and about the nature of the humanoid figure. Marcus explained that it was his mother, expressing pride in him and assuring him of her eternal presence. Ethan comforted Marcus, expressing their pride as well and apologizing for his earlier ego during their fight.

Marcus acknowledged his mistake and smiled, saying, "No need to be sorry. It was my mistake, too. I shouldn't have acted that way."

Lily looked at Ethan and asked, "Was that tough?" Ethan smiled.

Emily helped Marcus stand up and asked, "Where did you go this morning?"

Marcus explained, "Last night, my sleep was troubled. I had a strange dream where I saw an underwater monster being attacked by another creature on the ocean floor, causing the ocean volcano to erupt which caused a massive wave on the surface."

Taking a pause, Marcus hesitated to share that in one of his other dreams, he was fighting Ethan in their dinosaur and owl forms. As he had just sorted things out with Ethan, he chose not to reveal this detail.

Curious, Emily inquired, "What happened next? Did the monster survive?"

Marcus replied, "I am not sure, I woke up before finding out. But upon waking up, an angel spoke to me. It instructed me to leave the wall and go to a specific location. Not wanting to cause unnecessary worry, I didn't mention the angel's voice to you. The voice asked me to walk alongside the wall towards the east. It led me to a place near the ocean. When I reached the designated place, the voice guided me to sit and meditate. I was told to place the sword between me and the ocean, aligning its crystal with the center of my eyebrows. The voice advised me to focus on a single thought, which proved challenging. I kept getting distracted, mostly thinking about food. The voice suggested that I practice this daily to enhance my control over my power."

Ethan exclaimed, "Wait, there's an ocean nearby? I'm surprised we haven't ventured to the eastern side of our towns before."

Curious about the process, Lily asked, "Should I lay the sword on the ground and do a plank position with the crystal aligned to the center of my eyebrows?"

Ethan added humorously, "In that case, I should do the opposite—lie down on my back and place the sword on top of me. But knowing me, I might just fall asleep instead of meditating. Marcus, shouldn't you be flying over the ocean to precisely position the sword between you and the water?"

Marcus explained, "I suppose flying might have been an option, but the idea is to have one side of the sword facing you and the other side towards your element. It doesn't have to be positioned exactly in the middle."

Relieved, Lily responded, "Thank goodness! I can't even hold a plank for a minute. It feels like an eternity."

Emily redirected the conversation, saying, "Let Marcus finish his story before we delve into discussions. What happened next? Did you gain more power after the meditation?"

Marcus continued, "Not really. I struggled to sit for even ten minutes, and my mind was often distracted during that time. It seems mastering the ability to concentrate on a single thought for an extended period requires significant practice. I was about to head home and the voice instructed me to halt, just near the Dragoor's skull. The voice conveyed that the fate of my town rested in my hands. Initially, I didn't fully grasp it, but when I saw a massive amount of water heading towards our town through the hole in the wall, it became clear. I managed to divert most of the water, but my efforts fell short. Some water reached Ethan's part of the town."

Lily reassured Emily and Marcus, saying, "In case you're worried, we were evacuated to safety before the water struck. Fortunately, no one in our town was harmed."

Marcus continued, "After that, I attempted to redirect the water and push it out of the wall. Dragoor's skull was also pushed out in the process. As I was heading home, the voice took on a form floating in the air, and that's when you all arrived."

Ethan inquired, "Could the underwater monster fight be connected to the flood that hit our town?"

Lily added, "I think so too. Our dreams have come true before, right? This isn't the first time."

Surprised, Marcus asked, "What?"

Emily explained, "Yes, the three of us shared the same dream about meeting Margoor. It didn't unfold exactly as in the dream, but it happened."

Ethan shared, "Just a few hours ago, one of my dreams came true when I saw my professor, who had lost feeling in his legs, was suddenly able to walk and even ride a bicycle on his own near the river bridge."

Emily gasped, "His legs got better in the Call of Dream!"

Ethan nodded, "Yeah, it was amazing. In just forty days, he was walking again."

Lily, who had been studying how the body can heal itself with enough rest and a calm mind, added, "That's the incredible thing about our bodies. They're designed to fix a lot of problems by themselves if we give them the chance."

Marcus questioned, "So you're saying all dreams come true?"

Emily clarified, "Not all, I guess. I dreamed of flying over a forest, feeling the fresh breeze of the air, but with my powers, I can jump, not fly. But the question that's been bothering me is, why did you have a dream that didn't include you? Maybe it's just a dream then."

Lily added, "Yeah, maybe not all dreams, but most of them seem to happen in reality."

Marcus felt concerned about one of his dreams, thinking that he and Ethan might eventually have a conflict in their colossal beast form.

Ethan remarked, "Well, I suppose it's not too alarming. Your dream involved a monster, didn't it? At least our town wasn't directly affected. However, if even a distant monster battle in the ocean can bring such devastation to our towns, then perhaps it's time we consider improving our town's defenses."

Marcus, still thinking about the fight between him and Ethan in his dream, replied, "Yeah, I hope it's not much to worry about for now."

Lily suggested, "Can we do something?"

Ethan proposed, "Let's go explore the surroundings."

Lily looked at Ethan and countered, "I have something better in mind."

Lily plunged her sword into the ground and raised four cylindrical rocks, each reaching the height of an average person.

She asked, "Emily, in your dream, you said you were flying, right? Do you want to know what it feels like to fly?"

Emily, sensing Lily's plan might be dangerous, declined, "Ah… No thanks, I'm good. I might not want that dream to come true."

Lily insisted, "But today is your lucky day. I am going to make your dream come true. I suggest everyone hold onto the pillars like your life depends on it."

Emily, Ethan, and Marcus were terrified.

Ethan said, "I feel like this is not going to go well for me. First, let's discuss what you have on your mind."

Before Ethan could complete his sentence, Lily said, "Up we go," and began to raise the ground beneath them on which they were standing. The raised piece of ground was circular, with a diameter about the length of a bus. The four pillars that she had raised helped them from falling due to the vibration caused by the friction during the raising of the rocks.

While she was raising the rock, Ethan closed his eyes tightly, as he was not a big fan of heights. The rock kept rising and it felt like it was going up forever. Emily and Ethan began praying for the universe to change Lily's mind and bring them safely back to the ground. However, Lily didn't pay heed to their words. After a few seconds, the raising of the rocks stopped.

Marcus was not affected by the event, he was admiring the view. Emily and Ethan slowly opened their eyes. Emily got used to the height and was mesmerized by the scenery. On the other hand, Ethan clung to the pillar due to his fear of heights.

They observed their town which was very near the coast, with a lot of forested areas to be seen. The river Nivara connected to a lake, at the bottom of a mountain outside the wall, and they could see the exact boundary of the magic wall. Both Marcus and Emily thanked Lily for the view, while Ethan, lying on the edge of the raised rock, felt nauseous.

From that height, overlooking the forest beyond the mountain range of Nerupunila inside the magic wall, Emily noticed some movement. A glint of gold mixed with black caught her eye as it moved through the forest.

She strained to focus on the movement, but it quickly vanished beneath the dense leaves of the trees. She could not recall any animal with a black and gold skin color. Scanning the area, she found no further signs of activity. She considered mentioning it but decided to leave it undiscussed as Ethan distracted her.

Ethan exclaimed, "I am vomiting due to the height, and the height is making me vomit!"

Emily said to Lily, "Take us down. Looks like he can't handle the height."

Lily looked at Emily without saying anything.

Emily asked, "Why are you looking at me like that?"

Lily said, "Guess I did not think this through clearly."

Marcus asked, "What do you mean?"

Lily said, "I am sorry, Ethan. But I do not know how to bring us down."

Ethan looked at her in shock and jokingly told Emily to take care of their parents, as he might not be making it back to the ground.

Lily started creating circular steps for the raised pillar, allowing them to step down. She could only pull the steps one by one, and it took about an hour for the four to descend amid Ethan's plea for help. Descending was tougher for Ethan, as he had to look down each time he stepped down. So, he turned the other way around and descended backward.

Going down the lower half of the pillar was easier for him as the altitude decreased. The first thing Ethan asked for after getting down was to ask for water as he lay flat on the ground. Lily rushed to get water, but two people, who were already in the perimeter, delivered it to them. As Ethan drank the water, Marcus laughed.

Everyone looked at Marcus, thinking he was mocking Ethan for his state. Marcus immediately clarified that he was not trying to mock Ethan but rather pointing out how earlier they did not want water, and now all they needed was water. He highlighted that it was a perfect example of the phrase he had heard: "Too much of anything is good for nothing." The four realized the deep meaning of that phrase and felt enlightened.

Chapter 14

What is that Smell in the Air?

They returned home and from the next day onwards, they continued to explore the world outside the wall in pairs, taking turns. They all practiced their meditation to see if they could improve their powers. Days passed, and one day, Ethan couldn't find Lily anywhere. He searched all the possible places but couldn't find her. As it got darker, Ethan lost hope of finding her, thinking she might have gone outside the wall. However, a person pointed him in a direction, and he found Lily sitting on a bench in a park, looking at the sunset.

Ethan approached her slowly, and as he got close, he saw Lily wiping her tears. Ethan sat beside her and asked why she was sitting there alone.

Lily said, "It has been almost four months. Yet the Call of Dream has not stopped. I am worried about my mother. I am worried that I might not hear her voice again."

Ethan moved close to Lily to comfort her, putting his arm around her and allowing her to lean on his shoulder.

Lily said, “I do not understand. We fought the darkness the first week the Call of Dream began. I thought the magic wall had to be rebuilt and that is why the Call of Dream was prolonged. But there is no sign of any alien life coming to help us rebuild the magic wall. Why is this not ending?!”

Ethan, too, pondered the reason behind the delay. The things he wished for before the Call of Dream came into reality. The environment was clean and his love was beside him. Even the things he did not ask for were provided to him. But he felt something was missing. He could not figure out what it was exactly.

Lily saw Ethan sitting thinking about something deep and apologized for pushing her burden on him. Lily said, “I am sorry. Sometimes, I find myself being emotionally vulnerable.”

Ethan said, “Oh, don’t say that. You are not emotionally weak. You are just human. This is who we are. You have to be sorry only if you do something wrong. There is nothing wrong with hoping to hear your mother’s voice. If you think you are dumping your burden on me. You are wrong again. It is not a burden to me. It is my responsibility to take care of the person I love.”

Lily was surprised when Ethan confessed his love for her. Lily immediately asked, "Did you say you love me?"

Ethan was stunned by her question. Ethan, taken aback, clarified what he had just spoken. He smiled as he realized that he referred to Lily as the person he loved. Ethan cleared his thought and said, "I had been practicing this in front of the mirror a thousand times. Let me see if that is helping me now."

He prayed to the universe before beginning. He said, "Lily. The moment I look into your eyes. I forget everything, literally everything. The thousand times I practiced in front of the mirror is not helping me. Your smile makes me think about nothing else. I feel powerless when I look into your eyes. You help me with building my confidence and force me to be a better person. From this point onwards, there are going to be just words coming out of my mouth. I am just going to blabber some…"

Lily kissed Ethan, and it was everything he could have wished for. Just a few months ago, he might not have believed he'd be sharing such a moment with Lily. Despite its imperfections, Ethan's words were precisely what Lily needed.

Life often teaches us that in the pursuit of perfection, we can miss out on precious moments. Nobody is perfect, just like me, the author, sometimes drifting away from the story and giving you, the reader, advice you've heard a thousand times.

When Ethan opened his eyes after the kiss, he found himself in his bed. The experience felt real, and he could not believe it was a dream. Determined to understand what happened, he quickly got ready and went to find Lily to see if she had a similar dream.

As he headed downstairs, his father stopped him, questioning his rush. His mother joined in, asking if he felt different that morning. To Ethan's surprise, his parents were engaged in a normal conversation, not exhibiting the unusual behavior from the Call of Dream. He heard a dog barking outside his house. Birds were chirping all around. It seemed like the Call of Dream was over, and his parents had no memory of it. They expressed feeling better and more energetic.

His father said, "I feel young again. Surprisingly, my body ache has disappeared. I can move faster. What did we eat yesterday?"

His mom said, "It was the usual. But we did not eat much as we were discussing Emma's condition. I wish she felt better like us."

His father asked, "So you are saying that since we did not eat much last night, we are feeling a difference in energy? Ethan, how are you feeling? Aren't you feeling the difference like us?"

Ethan with a doubt in his mind said, "I mean. I feel everything is… normal." He meant to say, "Everything is back to normal, but held back."

His father looked at his mother and said, "It's probably the less food. So, Ethan, where were you rushing off to in that dress? You usually don't wear them while going outside, right?"

Ethan realized that he was in his comfortable clothes which might not be suitable for the outdoors. He was not yet ready to unveil the truth to his parents as he thought that he had been dreaming about the whole Call of Dream. To avoid the attention he said, "I just thought of getting some fresh air."

His father said, "OK then. Get on with it. I am going to try and see how many push-ups I can do!"

As Ethan stepped outside, he noticed everyone walking and running normally, excited about their improved health. People in the street were discussing the mysterious events from the previous night, attributing the positive changes to some unknown occurrence.

After a few minutes, both his parents came out of the house, holding their hands, laughing, and smiling at each other.

Ethan asked, "So, Dad. How much were you able to do?"

His father said, "Oh, only once."

Ethan asked, "With all that energy, were you able to do only one push-up? I was expecting at least five."

His father said, "Five in a day! I don't think I can do that. Maybe one more after some time. That is all my body can handle."

His father and mother looked at each other and giggled. Ethan asked, "Are we still talking about push-ups?"

His father changed the discussion topic by asking, "Oh, what is that smell in the air?"

Ethan could not, but his mother noticed a difference in the air, realizing it was the smell of fresh and clean air. His mother, excited about the change, remarked that the entire town seemed to be experiencing the same positive transformation. It was as if they had slept a year back and awakened in an improved world.

Curious about the gathering of people, they discovered a six-year-old boy named Kural sharing his experiences. He mentioned that his parents had stopped talking to him, he had not been going to school, and people were walking with their hands raised. The boy described hearing monstrous sounds and seeing water everywhere.

While some dismissed it as a mere dream and some praised his creativity, Ethan sensed that the boy was recounting genuine experiences. He remembered seeing the boy walking down the street with his hands raised, an image etched in his memory from the first time he peeked out of his window to witness people meditating in the Call of Dream. Ethan doubted that the boy, like himself, was not affected by the Call of Dream and was simply imitating those he had observed on that particular day when Ethan saw him.

As the crowd dispersed, Ethan's curiosity about the boy grew. He approached him and asked, "How long have you been seeing people walking with their hands up?"

Being only six, Kural hadn't counted the days. "Lots and lots," he replied. Then, out of the blue, he said, "I saw you turn into a big owl and fight a white creature named Vangoork."

Ethan was taken aback. He hadn't seen Kural during the fight with Vangoork, so he was surprised to hear Kural mention it. He couldn't fathom how Kural knew about the creature's name. "How do you know that? Did you watch us fight?" Ethan asked.

"I saw it in my dream," Kural replied.

Before Ethan could ask more questions, Kural's mother whisked him away. Just before leaving, Kural flashed a smile at Ethan and called him "Twinkle Toes."

The mention of the nickname transported Ethan back to his childhood when his grandmother used to call him that. He remembered how he would play with glitter, leaving a trail of it wherever he went. Speechless, he pondered how Kural knew about the nickname that was known only to his family. His thoughts were interrupted as his parents excitedly pulled him away, discussing their newfound flexibility.

With the Call of Dream seemingly over and people questioning the changes that could not have occurred overnight, Ethan was unsure whether to share the details of what had happened with everyone.

In the evening, a heartwarming surprise awaited them. Lily and her parents visited Ethan's house with good news. However, Ethan felt his heart break as Lily did not seem to notice him at all. He was worried that she might not remember anything that happened during the Call of Dream. They all gathered in the living area, and Emma spoke up, saying, "All my worries have disappeared. I am completely cured."

Ethan's mom was surprised and exclaimed, "Are you telling the truth?! How did this happen?"

Emma explained, "I am not sure. Yesterday, after I left your house, I went straight to bed without having my dinner. Today morning, I woke up feeling energetic, like how I was during my college days. It was weird, so we all went to the doctor. The doctor was even more shocked than us after he took some tests. He said it was not possible. And the exact words he used were…"

Emma looked at her husband, who said, "Medical miracle."

Emma continued, "The doctor said that I am perfectly alright now. It was like I was not even sick in the first place. Maybe it was the burden that was making me feel worse. As soon as I spoke to you both yesterday, I felt healed."

The atmosphere in the living room was joyful. While Ethan was happy that Lily's worries were solved, he also felt a tinge of sadness, realizing that Lily seemed to have forgotten the events of the Call of Dream. As his parents and Lily's parents caught up on the stories they had missed during their disagreement, Ethan quietly stood up to leave for his room.

Emma saw Ethan leaving and stopped him, saying, "Ethan and Lily, aren't you both going to the same class? Don't mind us old bags, you guys can do something while we catch up on our stories."

Ethan replied, "I was just about to head upstairs to my room."

Lily stood up and said, "I'll join Ethan. I have something to discuss with him." So, both Ethan and Lily headed upstairs.

Lily began, "I wanted to discuss the environmental protection thing I was asking for volunteers for at college yesterday."

Ethan was hoping Lily would talk about the Call of Dream, but as she did not, he worried that he had to start talking with Lily from scratch. He reassured himself that

Lily was the love of his life, so he could do anything to win her back. He thought to himself, "How hard could it be compared to a math test?"

Lily mentioned that even though she asked for volunteers, their town doesn't need saving because it's already way better than the day before. As Lily spoke the last few words, she winked at Ethan.

Confused, Ethan did not understand the meaning of the wink. Lily whispered to him, "How's my acting? Did I sell it?"

Ethan took a deep breath, relieved that Lily remembered the events of the Call of Dream. He said, "It was breathtaking!" They shared another kiss, and then Lily checked her surroundings, but everything seemed normal.

She mentioned, "I thought our kiss had some unique weird powers. I thought the Call of Dream ended because we kissed and I thought it might begin again if I kissed you. I'm relieved it doesn't. I can kiss you whenever I want."

Ethan felt like the happiest man in town. He said, "I'm very happy to know that your mother's illness is cured."

Lily nodded, "Yeah. Before we kissed, I was wondering why the Call of Dream didn't stop. Maybe it was to help people with their health problems. Lately, we haven't been eating well, and the air around us is polluted with dust. I read a report recently that said pollution-related diseases have been increasing a lot in recent years. Just look at the examples: our professor's legs are working again, and my mom's heart disease is gone. I'm starting to think the Call of Dream wasn't just to keep us safe from dangers outside the wall but also to heal the harm we've done to ourselves."

Curious, Ethan asked, "Do you know what happened when we kissed?" Lily admitted, "No idea. After the kiss, I was at home in my bed." Ethan added, "I don't remember what happened after the kiss either. Could we have gone to the Call of Dream as well?"

Lily exclaimed, "We could have spent some time in the Call of Dream like the others!"

They heard a knock at their door, and Ethan and Lily went downstairs to answer it. However, Ethan's father had already opened the door, and he stood there without saying anything. Ethan's mother, curious about the visitor, joined them. Ethan went to the door and found Marcus holding an old cloth – the clothes Emily had been wearing since she disappeared.

Ethan's parents seemed shocked at the sight of Marcus, even though they should not have known him. At least, that's what Ethan thought. However, their parents were indeed surprised by Marcus, even before noticing the clothes he held.

Ethan's father said, "I can't believe my eyes."

Ethan's mother said, "You look just like you did twenty years ago, except your hair is a lot shorter now."

Confused, Marcus inquired, "Sorry, have you seen me before?"

Ethan's mother replied, "You are the reason we are alive. Twenty years ago, we were camping north of Mandrook with our two-year-old Ethan when some people attacked us, trying to rob us. They threatened to harm Ethan if we didn't give them our money. We were far from the town, and nobody could hear our cries for help. Just when we thought that our lives were about to end, you appeared and helped us."

Marcus said, "I don't remember that. Are you sure it was me?"

Ethan's mother continued with tears in her eyes, "We'll never forget the face with the long blond hair who saved us from the robbers and left without speaking a word after sniffing our hair."

Marcus awkwardly smiled. "Um… That doesn't sound like something I'd do."

Ethan's mother gazed at Marcus's eyes and said, "I'm certain it was you."

Ethan's father didn't like Marcus standing outside and invited him inside, but before entering, Marcus insisted that Ethan's parents take a look at the clothes he was holding. Ethan's mother immediately identified the clothes and began crying even more.

Ethan's mother inquired, "Where did you find this?"

Marcus replied, "Finding this dress wasn't the surprising part. Finding its owner is."

With those words, Marcus stepped aside, revealing Emily standing behind him. The sight left Ethan's parents speechless with joy. Their long-lost daughter, now a radiant young woman, stood before them.

Ethan's mother exclaimed, "You are our guardian angel!"

Marcus pondered to himself, "Hmm... Yeah. I am a guardian, and I am the son of an angel. I guess I could be a guardian angel."

Everyone settled in the living room. Lily's parents could not be happier, witnessing two miracles in a day. Ethan's parents expressed their gratitude to Marcus for saving their daughter and bringing her back home. Marcus tried to explain that he was not the one who saved Emily, but the family was more interested in the reunion. So Ethan suggested finding another time to share the details.

Recognizing the importance of honesty and family bonds, Lily and Ethan felt it was time to share the truth with their parents. They urged them to brace themselves for some startling revelations.

Ethan began hesitantly, "Given recent events, there might be confusion among all of you. We hope to provide clarity and answers to your questions. It's a lot to take in, but we've decided it's time to reveal the truth."

Taking a deep breath and glancing at Lily, Emily, and Marcus, he turned to their parents and continued, "It's called the Call of Dream…"

Chapter 15

Whistle Melody in the Beyond

In a place unknown and forgotten to beings living in the three-dimensional world of Gardoon, Garvil, who had just returned after spending about a thousand years in Gardoon in the form of a dinosaur named Kargoor, spoke, "You betrayed me."

Vaulmour, who had been living on Gardoon as Vangoork, replied, "I thought I was heading towards something better. But now I regret my actions. I feel guilty for what I've done."

Garvil said, "You desired to gain power and rule a world. A wish that led you to take a life form in that world. Moreover, influenced by your actions and love, I also made a mistake by listening to you. How do you feel now? Has your wish come true?"

Vaulmour apologized, "My wish came true. I ruled a part of Gardoon for about fifty years before my life ended. But I grew greedy and wanting to gain more power, I acted badly. I feel guilty. My actions were poor in nature."

Garvil stated, "Exactly. I've returned from my punishment, but you've added more to your punishments. Now, return to Gardoon, and let's see if you can empty your sins collected and revert to your old self to reclaim your position in my palace."

Vaulmour expressed gratitude, "Thank you for saving my soul from destruction."

Garvil stated, "Destroying souls is not my responsibility. You already know it, but I am just reminding you. I'm only here to guide the souls to become better. Start with a simple life form, improve yourself, learn from mistakes, and eventually take on a human form. When you prove your balance, you can come back."

Vaulmour inquired, "How long will it take for me to reclaim my position beside you and in your heart?"

Garvil responded, "Time is irrelevant in the journey of cleansing the soul. Just ensure you don't turn the world into a dark place like yourself. If that happens, my father might consider destroying the entire world, including the darkness within you, and starting anew. And speaking about a place for you in my heart. That position is not available for you. You betrayed me and caused me pain because of your selfishness."

Guided by another soul to become better, Vaulmour, who had realized her mistake, was sent back to Gardoon in the form of an ant.

Garvil had regained control over his palace and examined the events that occurred during his absence in the three-dimensional world of Gardoon. Reflecting, he murmured, "Seems like the darkness has already influenced the hearts of many beings in Gardoon. Now, it's in my hands to cleanse some of it."

Garvil's attention was demanded by a woman who entered his castle, dashing. Everyone was prepared to attack the woman, but she did not flinch even a little. From behind her, a soldier threw a spear with a sharp tip at her. The spear had a sharp Emsesqueer gem forged to its edge. The gem could make any soul in this universe remain still until the gem was removed from the soul. It struck the woman's soul but did not have any effect. The soldiers stood stunned as they had not seen any soul restrict the power of the Emsesqueer like her before.

In anger, the woman looked at Garvil and said, "Guess you have very good protection around you here, and seems like everyone around here has forgotten me."

Garvil told his people to stand down, saying, "Your attacks won't work against her. She is the bearer of the Phoenix soul stone. Your attacks will be in vain."

His soldiers lowered their weapons and returned to their post. As Garvil took out the spear from the woman's back, he said, "The guards are new here. They did not even recognize me. If not for my ministers, I would have been mistaken for a trespassing soul."

He returned the spear to the soldier who threw it, acknowledged him for his good work, returned towards the woman, and said, "Seems your curse is lifted, Mom."

Kaiya spoke, "I had to wait for 1200 years to be free. Wandering the three-dimensional world in that physical form was the most unpleasant thing I have ever done."

Garvil asked, "So, how was father's curse lifted?"

Kaiya spoke, "The atonement for my curse was for one of our family members to ask for a better life for me while my soul is released from the physical realm. I was hoping for my favorite son to come to save me. Why didn't you come?"

Garvil chuckled, "Did you think Father would have forgiven me for helping Vaulmour? I spent the last 1200 years down in Gardoon as well. We may have met back there but could not have known. What form were you in?"

Kaiya said, "A peacock."

Garvil stared at his mother and asked, "Really? A peacock? Father must have had a soft corner for you. For the things that you did during the darkness awakening, he should have done something much worse. Revealing the secrets of the magical beasts to the people of Gardoon. Teaching humans a forbidden magic to extract the power of the magical colossal creatures in Gardoon by killing them. I can continue for at least an hour, listing the things you did that Father told you not to. I thought he would have imprisoned you in a stone that gets stamped by all the creatures in that world. He only cursed ten percent of what I might have cursed if I was in his place.

A peacock, you said? And I was a dinosaur with a terrible smile."

Kaiya said, "Oh, come on. Do you think he did me a favor? Everyone knows you are his favorite. I am sure he must have had his reasons. Nothing happens here without a reason, as he makes sure everything is connected and has a purpose."

Garvil nodded in disagreement with her statement about him being his father's favorite. He asked, "So, what brings you here?"

His mother said, "I had to spend 1200 years without seeing all my children. Should I need any more reason to come visit my favorite son?"

Garvil, knowing his mother, asked, "He banished you from his palace, didn't he?"

His mother remained silent for a few seconds knowing that his son had figured that she did not have any other place to stay and with a quirky smile tried to change the topic of conversation by asking, "So, is it true that you have a son? Where is he? When can I meet my grandson?"

With deep sorrow in his heart, Garvil said, "You might have seen him too, down there."

His mother asked, "Why the long face?"

Garvil said, "He was born for me and an angel when we were in our dinosaur form in the physical realm. I am afraid that he will not be allowed here until his time on Gardoon is over."

His mother consoled him by saying, "It is not your mistake. If someone has to be blamed, it should be your father. Gods should have entrusted me with Gardoon, but they chose him. And like I said, it is your father we are discussing. He does things for a reason. Maybe the angel was sent for you to fall in love with her and bring your child to that world."

Garvil gazed at Gardoon, observing Marcus from his dimension. He remarked, "I hope you'll make Gardoon a better place."

As Garvil watched Marcus in Gardoon, he also saw Ethan and Lily beside him. Together, they examined a rose stem that had grown into a plant where Ethan had buried the golden peacock. Lily named the rose plant Goldleaf Aurarose.

As he prepared to resume his work, Garvil noticed something unusual happening in Gardoon. He heard a beautiful whistle melody coming from a higher dimension than his own. He recognized the tune immediately. It was Hanusamiran, one of the protectors of the Par galaxy in the Kan universe. Gardoon was a part of Par galaxy. Hanusamiran and Shivamina were twins, younger siblings of Garvil.

What intrigued him was that Ethan could hear music originating from a higher dimension in the lower dimension.

Garvil's smile widened as he realized what was happening, "So that's why Ethan could relieve me from my dinosaur form," he muttered to himself.

Curious about Garvil's sudden smile, Kaiya asked him about it. Garvil then inquired, "Do you remember what happened when you died?"

Kaiya nodded, "Yes. There was a creature named Vangoork that went rogue and began killing all the peacocks in Gardoon. I don't recall creating that creature with pitch-black eyes. Maybe your father and sister, Ira, had something to do with that creature. I managed to evade it for a long time, but one day, its eyes caught me. It had somehow obtained one of the swords of Zingburg and was attempting to control my mind. However, being a superior soul, I was strong enough to restrict its mind-control attempts. It was not the same case with my physical three-dimensional peacock body, it was weak. I fought against that creature, but I was almost defeated and badly injured. I barely escaped and felt like I had lost control of my body. When I regained my strength, I found myself in a town where people were walking with their hands raised. That's the last thing I remember."

Garvil continued, "That town you found yourself in is Mandrook, which is surrounded by an invisible magic wall."

Kaiya nodded, saying, "I've heard of that town. Ira mentioned it and something called Call of Dream."

Garvil explained, "The people of the town you saw were controlled by Zendayan to save them from themselves. That's why they had their hands raised under the Call of Dream. You were also under his influence. He guided you inside the invisible magic barrier. After your passing, your peacock body was buried there, and a person named Ethan wished for a better life for you."

Curious, Kaiya asked, "Who is Ethan? Is he a family member? And how did he break my curse?"

Garvil replied, "Ethan is an incarnation of Hanusamiran. He was the one who freed my soul from my dinosaur form. Father cursed me, saying I'd stay in that form until he sent his blood to free me with a weapon he forged himself. I searched everywhere on Gardoon for that weapon but found nothing. Now, looking back, I understand. The weapon that Father forged was always with me, inside me, since the day I arrived in Gardoon. He hid the sword in the one place I'd never think to look."

Kaiya asked, "Where are Hanusamiran and Shivamina? It's been thousands of years since I last saw them. I remember the day they left for a higher dimension as per God's request. I haven't seen them since then. They weren't in the War of Nalvil, and they weren't there during our judgment either."

Garvil explained, "They fought in the war, but both had to give up their powers to protect the worlds from darkness. God asked them to be reborn in each world to safeguard them from danger."

Curious, Kaiya suggested, "Can't you lend them your Paasa stone so they can travel between dimensions?"

Garvil glanced at his mother and joked, "Why? So, Dad can send me back to Gardoon to live as a dinosaur again? You know your husband doesn't like us getting personally involved with Gardoon. I thought I was your favorite."

Kaiya reassured him, "I was just concerned about them. I thought you might be able to help."

Garvil replied, "Don't worry too much. They're the protectors of all the worlds in the Par galaxy. God didn't choose them for no reason. They're much better at handling things than we are."

Kaiya then asked, "And what about Shivamina? Is she also incarnated in Gardoon?"

Garvil confirmed, "Yes, she is. When I was back in Gardoon as Kargoor, I felt like I knew Emily and Ethan. Now I understand why I felt that way."

Finally, Kaiya asked, "Is our world out of danger?"

Garvil explained, “For now, our world is safe. But there’s a looming danger in Gardoon. It seems that the portals from Gardoon to the other worlds in Par are opened again. If we don’t deal with it, Gardoon could face massive destruction. I was just about to head back there to handle the problem.”

Curious, Kaiya asked, “Is Vaulmour the danger you’re talking about?”

Garvil clarified, “No, Vaulmour was Vangoork in Gardoon, the creature you fought. She returned here, but her soul wasn’t pure, so I sent her back. She’s not the danger, but she was about to cause trouble along with another creature named Darnhull. They were planning something worse, but Vaulmour changed her mind and went after an artifact hidden in Mandrook and Koodam instead. That change of plan saved most of Gardoon. I wonder who prompted her to target those places for the artifact. Now that Vangoork is gone, Darnhull might proceed with the original plan. I need to hurry and stop it.”

Concerned, Kaiya asked, “Are you going alone? Remember what happened last time you listened to Vaulmour’s words, which brought a soul back to this dimension? You were reborn as a dinosaur. Can’t you ask Hanusamiran and Shivamina to help?”

Garvil explained, “It’s a bit tricky. Hanusamiran and Shivamina are in a deep meditative trance. It lets them send part of their soul to be born in the physical world. In this state, nobody here can talk to them. Even if Ethan and Emily knew about Darnhull, they wouldn't be able to stop it, even with Marcus, Lily, and all the swords of Zingburg."

Kaiya cautioned Garvil to carefully consider his decision, especially since it involved the Gods and higher beings. She warned, "Unlike your father, his superior Gods don't go easy on punishments."

Garvil retorted, "Easy on punishment? It was for you, not for me. And I've thought this through. If I don't stop Darnhull, the beautiful creations that you and Ira made will be destroyed."

Further in the Chronicles of Gardoon

Far away in Gardoon, distant from Mandrook and Koodam, a human named Doomdruk spoke to another human, Munloori. "I knew Vangoork wouldn't complete the task I gave it. What about Darnhull? Did it succeed?"

Munloori replied, "I don't have information on Darnhull, my lord. But I have a good feeling it will succeed. Darnhull is much more capable than Vangoork."

Doomdruk said, "We must harness the power that's been hidden from us for centuries."

Munloori agreed, "Yes, my lord. Only then will the Sun rise on our side."

Doomdruk then asked, "Have you captured the golden black dragon?"

Munloori lowered her head and admitted, "No, my lord. We still can't track it. The last Henosaur that encountered the beast said it disappeared into thin air near a waterfall."

Doomdruk asked, "Disappeared, you say. Hmm... that power could be useful for me, don't you think?"

Munloori, knowing what was coming, kept her head down and said, "Yes, Lord."

Doomdruk rose from his throne and walked toward Munloori. He drew his sword of Zingburg and placed it on her neck. "Then tell me, why are you here?"

Munloori replied, "My Lord, nothing is going as planned. Positivity is spreading its wings in Gardoon."

Doomdruk sighed. "I already know that. But I'm still not hearing a reason to not slit your throat."

Munloori took a deep breath. "We must wake Fronketta from its sleep. It's the only creature that can help us reach our goals quickly."

Doomdruk chuckled, removed the sword from her neck, and said, "I was considering the Doom of Namoor, but Fronketta doesn't sound bad. Plus, the Doom of Namoor might not be ready for a few years. You have my attention. Speak."

***

Marcus woke up from his dream again—the same one where he fought Ethan in their dinosaur and owl form. Wanting to calm his mind, he went to the ocean, planted his sword on the ground between him and the water, and sat down to meditate.

Just three minutes into his meditation, he heard a voice. He wondered if it was an angel. Suddenly, he sensed some movement in the ocean. Something was coming toward him. He grabbed his sword, ready to face whatever it was. He didn't feel afraid, he was confident he could use the water around him in the fight.

The waves grew larger and stronger, and then a colossal creature rose from the ocean. Marcus quickly created ice needles and aimed for the creature's eyes, but to his surprise, the ice turned back to water before hitting it and did not harm the creature at all. Confused, he tried again, but it ended in the same result.

He tried everything he could to stop the creature, but nothing worked. The creature didn't even flinch. Fear began to grip Marcus, and he transformed into his dinosaur form, charging at the creature. As he ran, he heard the voice again say, "Wait."

But it was too late to stop. The creature moved its head to the left, and a huge wave of water hit Marcus, throwing him several meters to the side.

***

Lily was worried because Ethan and Emily, who had left town three weeks ago, still hadn't returned. But she had bigger problems to deal with: a colossal white rhino was threatening Mandrook and Koodam.

In her white elephant form, Lily went into musth and started rampaging through the twin towns. Without Ethan and Emily, Marcus couldn't calm her down. All his attempts failed, and Lily ran out of Mandrook into the wild.

***

Marcus heard a call for help that only he could hear. An angel instructed him to find the soul that was crying out, saying it needed his help. Following his intuition, Marcus left town and began his journey.

As he traveled, the voice grew stronger, guiding him. After a couple of days, he felt the voice getting closed and stronger, calling to him one night. It was raining heavily, and the moon was hidden behind clouds, making it hard to see.

Sensing something nearby, Marcus didn't want to take any chances. He transformed into a dinosaur, gaining a higher vantage point. In a flash of lightning, he saw a human with two large horns kneeling on the ground, crying and looking up at the sky. The person hadn't noticed Marcus yet.

Just as Marcus was about to reveal himself, he saw a girl with wings spread wide, standing in the distance and facing him. He was stunned.

Glossary

Anabelle - Ethan's sister and Marcus's girlfriend

Crockabill - Green colossal creature on which Vangoork used for traveling

Devarnams - God-like beings, protectors of Gardoon

Dragoor - 900-year-old rivalry of Kargoor

Ella Watson - Lily's mother

Emily - Ethan's sister

Emma Soleman - Ethan's mother

Emsesqueer gem - A gem that could make any soul in this universe remain still until the gem was removed from the soul.

Ethan Soleman - Protagonist

Garvil - Purifier of Souls

Henosaur - White creature family that tastes like chicken

Kan - Universe in which Gardoon is part of

Kaiya – Thiarral's wife, Creator of life in Gardoon

Kargoor – A fire-breathing colossal being

Koodam - The town where Anabelle and Marcus live

Lily Watson- Ethan's love interest

Mandrook - The town where Ethan and Lily live

Margoor – A giant luminous butterfly

Narad – A ttraveler across universes

Nerupunila – A mountain Range

Nivara – A river flowing through Mandrook and Koodam

Paasa stone – It lends one the ability to travel between dimensions

Phoenix soul stone - A stone that Kaiya possesses

Sargoor - A blue creature about half the size of Kargoor, which Kargoor named Sourtail

Sebastian - An old man who lives in Mandrook

Swords of Zingburg – Magical swords that possess magical powers.

Thiarral - The head of Devarnams of Gardoon

Thomas Soleman - Ethan's father

Vangoork – A white human-like creature with black eyes.

Vaulmour - Garvil'a first love

Wolftahs - Small yellow creatures size of a dog

www.ingramcontent.com/pod-product-compliance
Lightning Source LLC
LaVergne TN
LVHW041156150826
845673LV00001B/183

9798893632859